A Tale of
TWO
SPARROWS

VANESSA FOWLER

Cover by Luisa Galstyan
Map art by Vanessa Fowler

ISBN Hardcover: 979-8-9999167-0-9
. ISBN Softcover: 979-8-9999167-1-6

Library of Congress Control Number: 2025919891

Published by Every Day Deeds Press
Honolulu, HI

For Max, Maile, Skye, and Cruz,
I love you with all my heart.

Saint Michael
Saint Selaphiel

"Are not two sparrows sold for a penny?
Yet not one of them will fall to the ground outside your Father's
care. And even the very hairs of your head are all numbered.
So don't be afraid; you are worth more than many sparrows."

Matthew 10: 29-31

Chapter 1
Colin

The Duke and I wind our way down a long stone staircase. My mentor is silent, and as his shadow swallows me up, sweat trickles down my back. He stops when we arrive at a wooden door, barely visible within the soot-stained wall. I bring the flame of my torch closer to the concealed entryway. The wood is engraved with leafy trees and a herd of reindeer that, in the quivering flickers of light, appear to be staring right at me. My pulse quickens, and I'm drawn closer to the image.

"Hold still." The Duke hands me his torch.

He pulls out a chain from around his neck with several iron keys strung on it. The simplicity of the one he selects to push into the door tells me it would be easy to pick this lock. Inside, the space is taller and deeper than the entryway would have suggested. A long table sits in the middle of the room, and tapestries drape the walls. How many secret Keeper meetings have been held here over the centuries?

The Duke lifts one of the hangings—a hunter who has caught a pheasant in a big net—and reveals a cabinet. He selects the second key. This one is pretty basic, too, for what it's guarding. The cabinet shelves are lined with rows of the blue-glass flasks filled with the priceless protective concoction, the Remedy—a drug only permitted for our Keepers, the guardians of our cities.

The Duke hands me one of the flasks and takes another for himself.

"Here's to your father," he says, raising his Remedy in a toast.

My heart pounds hard. Have I earned this?

"To my father." I bring the drink to my lips. The liquid has an unexpected fragrance, like warm caramel and melted butter. The soothing scent steadies me. My shoulders relax, and I drink. I close my eyes to savor the flavors—decadent, like cream, apricots, and a festival of wonders. As the Remedy's warmth courses through me, before I even realize what I'm doing, I crush the empty glass vial in my hands. Even the shards don't bother me.

The Duke's jaw juts out. "Let's go greet Sir Jasper," he says.

The Duke and I march back up to the courtyard, and there, a guard is waiting for us with our horses. Mine is a chestnut mare I named Lightning when I was twelve—my father gave her to me before he died. Her ears pin back when I approach.

"We are finally going into the wilderness together, like we always dreamed," I tell her as I stroke her face.

Her tail flips, and she shakes her head at me.

"Ready?" the Duke asks.

"Trust me," I tell Lightning, and she settles down.

We mount our horses and take the main road through the middle of the city, to the inner gate. It is already open, but the Keepers stationed there escort us—a necessary formality, since it's the Duke who is passing through. Then, we gallop ahead through the farmlands to the second wall. At this time of year, the harvest is wrapping up, so the fields we cross are barren.

The outer gate glows by the light of dozens of fiery torches and spears. At least a dozen guards work to pull up the iron bars and unfasten the massive wooden doors that protect our city from the creatures. Now, we will be the ones guarding the city.

"You have one goal out here. Prove yourself," the Duke says. "Destroy any creatures if they appear. And know they are out there, watching, even if you cannot see them."

My jaw tightens, and I sharpen my focus on what lies ahead. Outside, from the endless forests, the caravan of lights approaches. Though not small, it appears minuscule compared to the forest. It has arrived from Saint Selaphiel, with provisions and food. At the front of the escort is Sir Jasper, the current Head Keeper.

Even from this distance, I can tell when he notices me. The old man's sharp eyes lock onto mine, and his expression hardens. He shakes his head in disapproval. I'm tempted to smile at his reaction. He reminds of my horse.

I turn my attention past the Head Keeper, to the Ruler in her elaborate carriage. She's the one who matters, and I can tell she's waving at us through the side window.

As the caravan advances closer to the fortifications, a commotion breaks out behind us. It takes me a moment to work out what's happening, but it appears a dozen or so agriculturalists have come through the gate and are rushing to greet the caravan.

"Shouldn't we stop them?" I ask.

The Duke lifts his hand and signals me to stay put. "This is their choice. We cannot compromise the safety of the caravan for them."

What are these agriculturalists doing? How could they be this foolish?

Just as the people approach the woods, something like a massive, violent dust cloud overtakes them, with flashes of red eyes and the silhouettes of large, dark beasts barely perceptible, yet visible. As they are enveloped, the agriculturalists scream and run.

"Let's go," the Duke orders as he rides forward.

There is no turning back now, and I break into a gallop after him. I'm grateful for the Remedy, because I think I could face anything right about now.

"Let's see who wins today: you or the creatures," the Duke says as I catch up to him.

My grip on the reins tightens. That's not a gamble I can afford to lose.

When we come closer to the caravan, he grabs two flaming spears and hands one to me.

"Go after them," he shouts. "If you pierce one with fire, you win." Then, he weaves in and out of the caravan with his flames, presumably scaring away the creatures, and he leaves me to my own devices.

Fingers tight around my fiery weapon, I gallop for the part of the forest the agriculturalists disappeared into. From under the hood of my cloak, I search for movement between the trees. The wounded bodies are like rags on the forest floor, and by the eerie whimpering and sounds of pain, some of them are still alive.

A woman cries at the base of a tree ahead of me. Her brown hair, smothered with dirt and blood, is plastered over her face. Her eyes interrogate me, scared and helpless.

I should keep moving, except her hurt compels me to her. I should be alert to the creatures, not the people—like the Duke said—but the reality is I cannot bring myself to continue on without attending to her.

While holding the flaming spear in one hand, I check my satchel for bandages and alcohol—standard Keeper fare. Then, after easing off Lightning to kneel beside her, I clean her wound.

"I know who you are," she says, her tone abrasive and her body rocking in pain.

"I'm here to help you. Why did you come out here?" I try to make my voice gentle, but it comes out with a bit of an edge.

"We thought it was safe," she says.

"Why would you think it was safe?"

"We thought the Keepers would protect us." Her eyes look at me pleadingly.

I finish bandaging her and help her adjust herself back up against the tree. I'm not sure what will come of her, but this is all that's in my capacity to do.

As I ease away, a rustling stirs the ground cover nearby. She hears it, too, because she grabs hold of my forearm and squeezes.

"I'm scared," she says.

"I'll protect you," I say. "But to do so, I need you to let go."

I loosen her fingers from my arm and search the surrounding forest for movement. I step past other survivors, flaming spear ready, listening for any more sounds. Several agriculturalists who lie there seem far gone—vacant stares, angry glares, or babbling to themselves. Where are the creatures?

An older man is crawling on the ground. Leaves and twigs stick out from his hair and beard. Deep scratches run across his clothes and back, but by the way his clear eyes call out to me, he doesn't seem as bad as the others.

More rustling. I search for where the sound came from and prepare my spear. I am ready.

"Come face me," I shout, as if the creatures could understand me.

The man on the forest floor shakes his head and drags himself away on his hands and knees, more animal-like than human. He scoots to a tree like it's his only hope of escape.

Right behind him, I glimpse something else. From among the trees, strange eyes are glued to me, red and yellow like fire. Is it waiting for me to leave these people for it to consume its prey? Or maybe, is it hungry for *me*? The creature's stare floods me with incomprehensible grief, fear, and horrible memories. Why do I feel like this? Isn't the Remedy supposed to give me strength against them?

I square my shoulders and begin to aim my flaming spear, ready to throw it, but freeze. Those eyes are paralyzing me with doubt. I am my own worst enemy. It's not the creature that is responsible for all this, it's me.

The man beside me shrieks, and the creature lunges for me. Just in time, a blazing arrow flies, hitting the outline of the creature. Its eyes extinguish and disappear.

Sir Jasper rides up beside me. "You are not safe here. Go home."

I am not quite aware of what is happening, but the Head Keeper helps pull me back onto my horse. I don't want anything to do with this man. He was the one who would have allowed my parents' murderer to go free. He is the one who opposed me entering the Keeper contests. But didn't he just save me?

As I start back out of the forest, the woman I bandaged is still leaning up against the tree, where I left her.

"Do you want to go back with me?" I ask her.

She nods and reaches her arms out to me. So, against all logic, I dismount and carry her toward Lightning.

"What are you doing?" the Duke shouts as he rides toward me. "These fools are better off without their own torment."

His face is flushed, and without warning, he yanks the woman from my arms. She screams as he pulls a knife from his side. His next swift action is terrible and deadly. Her life instantly leaves her.

"No!" I shout. I reach for her as she falls to the ground. What am I supposed to do now?

"She's better off this way," the Duke says. "Besides, there are consequences to breaking the law."

As he rides away, my world is shredding apart. Today, I was supposed to prove myself as a Keeper. Instead, I almost lost my life, and the one person I tried to help has been killed by my mentor.

The next thing I know, I'm back on Lightning, galloping through the gates. I cannot seem to grasp the Remedy's blanket of strength. It is ripping away.

CHAPTER 2
Molly

As I pull the braided wreaths of bread out of the glowing oven, the scents of burnt wood and baked grains saturate our little attic home—like my own version of a sacred incense.

Today is the day. The Keeper selections are what my brother and I have been training for our whole lives. If we make Keeper, our loyalty will be established—a Keeper oversees the safety of the cities, and so people won't question our trustworthiness anymore.

After they cool a little while, I arrange the breads in my sack and check on my twin brother. Hugo still appears peacefully asleep, but he most likely isn't either—asleep *or* peaceful. Below his semblance of stillness, there is like a surging, turbulent river, ready to overtake everything in its path at any moment.

After pulling on my boots, I wrap myself in my cloak, lowering its extra-large hood as best to conceal my burn-marked face beneath it. I slide through our trap door, down our thread of uneven, wooden stairs, and push the front door open. Outside, the dampness of decomposing leaves and oncoming rain permeates the air. A frosty forest wind whistles up the tight maze of mud and cobblestone paths and hits me. My bag of bread, at least, is nice and warm.

A woman's angry shouts echo through the labyrinth of passageways, over the rows of houses. My cue. I follow the sounds and find where the voice is coming from, then dig into my sack and bring out a wreath, wrap it in paper, place it on the front steps of the dwelling. After I knock on the door, I disappear into a shadowy nook across the way. If anyone sees me or figures out who I am, they will not want my gift. I cannot let that happen.

A lady opens.

"What?" The woman's voice, shaky and abrasive against the quiet of pre-dawn, makes me feel a tinge of ill. Her features are pinched, her cheeks sunken, and her eyes swollen. Will she even notice the bread?

"Who's out there?" she asks.

After searching the street to her right and left, she glances at the steps and reaches down for the wreath.

Deeper into the knot of twisting lanes, several young men hoist a beam through an upper-level window. A little girl stands, watching, with a brown dress—once with white flowers—and blushed cheeks, dark eyes.

I approach her, and she squints up at my face.

"For you and your family," I say, tucking a crusty bundle into her arms.

"Thank you," she says, in a hushed voice.

Before I can walk away, a too-skinny woman comes to stand in the entryway behind her. "Who are you talking to?" she asks.

The girl pulls the bread in closer.

As the woman eyes me, a gust of wind from beyond the walls shrieks through the alley and shifts the hood off my face. My heart squeezes, disappointment and shame ensnaring me. While my thick cloak and massive hood should keep me unrecognizable, fate, apparently, has other plans.

The woman yanks the little girl to her side.

"You're the Fitzpatrick girl, aren't you?" I guess she's already seen my scarring.

The young men pause their work.

My name and face are a curse in this city.

"No one wants your help," the woman continues, making it a point to address not only me, but her young audience.

She grabs the wreath from the girl's hands and tosses it to the ground, into the muck. It's hard to believe she just wasted so much valuable food.

"You don't deserve to be a contender." She spits on the destroyed bread. "No one is rooting for you. You have nothing in you of a Keeper."

A fog of numbness envelops me, yet from within it, hurt somehow still pulses within me. My mind is in a haze. Everything is blurry.

Move on, I tell myself. I know who I need to deliver my next wreath to. It's the most important one.

I pull my hood back over my face, hold the bag of remaining loaves close, and continue on.

CHAPTER 3
Colin

The storm in my mind intensifies as Lightning gallops through the gates of the outer walls and into the harvest lands. The fields and the caravan are an obscure blur, and I clutch my horse's mane, tighten the bridle, and urge her faster toward the inner-city gate ahead.

"Let me through," I shout at the guards.

Thankfully, they recognize me and allow me in. From there, Lightning continues at full speed through the busy streets—it's like she knows I'm desperate. A substantial ruckus follows in our wake as people scramble to make way.

When I make it to the locksmith shop I call home, my head drops into Lightning's warm, coarse hair. My body shakes and tears fall down my face. I need to find Uncle Felix, but then he is there, rushing in for me. I slide off my horse and, holding on to the wooden beams and fixtures near me, step forward to him.

"What happened?" Uncle Felix asks, examining my face.

I lower my head. I don't have words to explain.

Next thing I know, he holds me in his arms and guides me home. Inside, he leads me into his big leather chair and pours me a glass of water. When he hands it to me, my hand is trembling, and I spill it all over.

"Tell me what happened," my uncle says as he wipes me down, then helps me drink.

"Duke gave me Remedy, and I went with him to guard the incoming caravan. But there were agriculturalists, and we didn't help them. They were destroyed by the creatures. One of the creatures attacked me, too. I froze, and my soul would have been taken, but Sir Jasper saved me." I don't know if I'm making sense. What I do know is Uncle Felix's huge face is turning bright red.

"You took Remedy?" he says.

I nod.

My uncle grabs a broom and begins to sweep the shop floor, his motions jagged like a saw. Then, he dumps the sweepings into the hearth fire, causing sparks to fly.

"What about the regular Keeper training?" he asks. "I thought that's what you and the Duke were doing. *True Keepers*—like your father was—they didn't need Remedy. Sir Jasper doesn't teach his contenders to use Remedy. That's why you train to fight and be strong. You have to be able to fight creatures without Remedy. You have to fight them as *you*."

I don't want to listen to his lecture, but I owe it to him since he is the one who took me in after my parents died, and he is the one who is here, helping me now.

"But how could I ever train under Sir Jasper after he betrayed our family? Besides, he wasn't going to allow my selection for the Keeper contest. I wanted to tell you, but I didn't know how to. Only the Duke believes in me, and going out there yesterday was the only way to prove myself. I didn't want everything I've worked for—all my years of training—go to waste. But I completely failed, and I don't know what to think about the Duke or anyone, anymore."

"Sir Jasper protected you, didn't he? You should know what to think about him." Uncle Felix stares at me, and by the sharpness in his voice, he is very angry. "If you can talk to him, you might still stand a chance."

"Talk to him? How can you say that?" That's the last thing I can do, but by the burning look in Uncle Felix's eyes, I may not have much choice in the matter. "If he wasn't going to select me before, why would he ever select me now?"

"Sir Jasper might not select you to enter the contender contests, but you can at least start acting like a Keeper."

What does he mean by that?

"Don't give me that look," he says even though I'm not aware of having given him any look.

Not only is my mind still fracturing from the Remedy and everything that happened, but now Uncle Felix's words are like a punch in the gut. If I could stand and walk away, I would. I'm too weak though, so instead, I try to bring the cup of water to my mouth. But next thing I know, it slips from my shaking fingers, and the glass shatters all over the floor.

The three candles on my workbench have almost melted away, their light dim over my hands and tools. Yet, my mind continues storming. Like a malevolent slaver, it's shackled me in irons I can't seem to escape and my hands haven't stopped shaking. I've cut myself a few times, but this work of textures and puzzles and metal for Uncle Felix's box has been a shelter. Some special gift to family is a Keeper tradition, and I hope this one can help my uncle believe in me again.

My chisel slips again, and once more, I slice my finger. I wipe away the blood and stick my head out the window for some fresh air. Besides some scrapping cats, the street below is empty. After a little while, the cats scamper away, and a cloaked shadow approaches our shop. It must be Molly, because she pulls bread out from her bag, wraps it, sets it on our doorstep and rings the front bell. Before Uncle Felix can open up, she slinks into the shadows across the street so that no one can see her. Doesn't she realize we know it's her?

Her unwanted bread deliveries irk me, considering her father took my parents' lives. I would love for her to stop. Uncle Felix says it's her best at contrition for her family and that I should be more accepting. I don't think so. Though, after everything that happened to me recently, I empathize more with her humiliation.

I return to my worktable and once again examine each part of my uncle's lock box. Still thinking about Molly, I etch a few extra small details into the feathers and leaves of the design. I'm so angry with her family. If it weren't for them, my life would have been good. I would still have my parents. I wouldn't have been rejected by the Keepers. I wouldn't have almost just lost my soul to a creature. And now, I have to somehow talk to Sir Jasper—the one man I despise almost as much as the Fitzpatricks.

After I've polished and scrutinized my amalgamation of wood and metal once more, I wrap it in a piece of linen and blow out the already dying candles. I change my shirt, pulling on a thick one for warmth and a second one—the nicest one I own—for making the best impression I can. I line the inside of my leather boots with fresh goose feathers before pulling them on and ease my way down the creaky staircase into my uncle's locksmith shop.

As soon as I step onto the bottom floor, Uncle Felix pushes through the hanging locks, keys, and iron tools toward me, his belly jiggling under his apron, and Molly's bread under his arm.

He is studying me, and his eyes are tightening.

"Did you get any sleep?" he asks.

I shake my head no and push a hand through my mess of hair. "But I have a present for you," I say, with the best smile I can muster. "To honor Keeper tradition."

"You do?"

I shrug and hand him the wrapped-up lockbox.

He unfolds the cloth and, as he runs his thick fingers along the metal and wood mechanisms, his eyes glisten and his face lights up. Even the wrinkles around his eyes grow deeper than they already are.

"Can I try the key?" he asks.

"You need more than one," I say and pull the two keys out of my pocket.

"Two?"

I point him to the keyholes concealed under movable leaves. "For the both of us together. For family treasures."

"What family treasures?" Uncle Felix laughs.

I laugh uneasily with him. "Maybe ones we can try for?"

I place one of the keys in my uncle's palm, and together, Uncle Felix and I try the lock and keys, watching how the metallic leaves, branches, and birds work themselves open. With the first key, the leaves move to reveal the birds. With the second key, the birds tilt and the box opens.

"This is wonderful. I wish your parents could have seen this." Uncle Felix scruffs up my hair, messing it up more than it already is. Then, without warning, he pulls me in with his thick, soot-covered hands. He smells of cooked meat, metal, and fire—some of the best smells in all the world, I have to admit. If only I could cling to him and forget about everything else.

"No matter what happens today," Uncle Felix says, "just be the true Keeper you are meant to be."

After we let go, he hands me some dried beef from the pantry and a chunk of bread from the latest Molly delivery—I don't have the heart to turn it away—and wraps the food up in a waxed cloth. Once I fasten my black wool cloak over my shoulders, Uncle Felix gives me another hefty pat on the back. From there, I trudge through the passages that snake through Saint Michael, dreading the oncoming humiliation. Will Sir Jasper even talk to me? Plus, I'm sure word has gone out about what happened yesterday. By now, all the Master Keepers and many of the contenders will know what I did. Will anyone have anything to do with me?

Over the Straight Street Bridge, I stop to watch the river and eat some of the food from Uncle Felix. Though the intricate metalwork of the bridge usually inspires me, today, I can't help but wish I could be like the river and rush away. Only the wild River Trent has the luxury of running free, beyond the walls, cascading into the world beyond.

The truth is, the whole city is trapped in the grip of our heartless captors—the creatures—and their hunger is squeezing and crushing all of us. They've already destroyed five of our seven cities, and they are out there, stalking what remains of us. I thought I could be one of the ones to help protect us, but in the end, I'm just as helpless as those foolish agriculturalists.

For the first time, I take a bite of Molly's bread—I despised her and her brother for what their father did to my parents, but after what happened outside the walls, who am I to judge anyone? Who am I to refuse someone's kindness?

Stretching out in front of me, the earthy, gritty, and winding streets are dusted in the gentle gold of the approaching sunrise, and the tall spires of the Prince of Sparrows Cathedral stand out, bathed in the slivers of first light.

I sigh. Will the Keepers give me a second chance? And if not, what will I do?

CHAPTER 4
Molly

The water I lugged up last night is still freezing, but it cleanses me. I change into my favorite dress with its faded embroidered roses, reminders of the little girl from earlier. For a bit of cheering up, I weave a long length of velvet, sky-blue ribbon into my hair. I nibble on an apple slice from my satchel packed with food for later. I need the extra bit of sweetness.

Hugo is finally awake. He stands to warm his hands by the stove. I open the chest at the bottom of my mattress and pull out the sweater I knit him—my contender gift. I hope he likes it. He is always polished and well dressed, and I'm not sure if he'll feel this sweater will match him.

He holds my present up.

"Thanks," he says, threading it on. "It's perfect for a chilly day like today."

He has a glimmer in his eye and a grin on his face. "I have your gift, too. You didn't think I would forget, did you?"

Truth be told, with Hugo, I never know what to expect.

From under his bed, he hands me a wrapped package, clearly a book. Which one, and why he's so eager about it, I'm eager to see.

He nudges me when I take too long, and as I unwrap the bundle, a notebook engraved with an intricate winding tree emerges—familiar, but I can't place why. The branches of the tree continue to the top half of every page, growing, twining with detail and beauty, mingling with the text.

Something about this notebook unnerves me. As I continue to flip through the pages—thick, golden paper with brown and black ink that sometimes swirls together—I recognize the handwriting. It's our father's. I lift my eyes from the book to Hugo, and he nods to confirm my suspicion.

My hands tremble as fear courses through my insides, and I am overcome with the sudden urge to shove the pages in my brother's face.

Hugo's expression turns serious, and he places a hand on my shoulder. "I know you think you don't want it, but in this book is the answer to all our problems."

As I examine the notebook again, every muscle in my body tenses. My instincts warn me these pages hold the secrets to finding the lost Mirror of Sparrows, and that's why Hugo is so enthusiastic about them—but I'm not sure. The reality, however, is if this notebook is about the omniscient mirror—the Mirror of Sparrows—then the gift is a million times worse than anything I could have imagined. The information would be the result of our father's horrific greed and murderous actions. Doesn't

Hugo realize what he's doing? And today, on this day that was supposed to be so full of new possibilities?

"We have no right," I say. "Where did you find this?"

Has Hugo kept the notebook a secret from me for all these years? My heart pinches.

"We have every right, and this is our opportunity to make everything right." His face is taut with surprise. "Dad gave us this chance. He left this for us. This is ours."

How could Hugo and I feel so differently? This gift will not make everything right. On the contrary, it will be our seal of guilt.

I stare at my brother in silence. Should I keep this curse of a book secret from the Keepers? If I hand it in, I betray my brother. The Keepers will condemn him—not to mention still hate me for having had the book, as well. If I do not surrender the notebook, I betray the cities, and I become the very traitor and conspirator everyone says I am.

This is the worst gift ever.

Hugo and I cross the Straight Street Bridge and arrive at the wrought-iron gates of the Keeper Headquarters. What I'd hoped would be my portals of salvation feel like gates of doom. I decided bringing the notebook was the right thing to do, but at the moment, I'm no longer so sure. It's just a small notebook in my bag, but because of it, I want to run away and disappear. There is no turning back now, though. We are through the gates and past several guards. Ahead of us, several dozen contenders are already here, all of them waiting for the opportunity to further prove themselves.

Massive crimson banners drape the ornate stone buildings and courtyard walls. Garlands of red roses hang at the front. It's breathtaking. And, as the dawn bells toll, the Ruler enters. She has journeyed here from Saint Selaphiel, the only other surviving city in this forsaken wilderness. Her red silk gown, matching all the surrounding roses, floats around and behind her. Streams of ribbons adorn her hair, and golden cuffs and rings encrusted with rubies cover her arms and hands. She's a brilliant fighter, as well. She mesmerizes me—and everyone else around me, too.

Just as the Master Keepers line up around her at the top of the steps, the Ruler's eyes dart toward the courtyard gates. I follow her gaze to see Colin Kelly has arrived.

Everyone turns, not just because he's Colin Kelly, but because he wasn't supposed to be here today. Thanks to his family name and the Duke's favor, he's supposed to have bypassed the traditional Keeper selection process. Something must have happened. I'm curious to see how the Keepers—and especially Sir Jasper—will respond to him.

"Well, look who decided to show up," Hugo says. He despises Colin just as much as Colin despises us—though to say that Colin despises us is too kind. Since our father murdered his parents, we are non-existent to Colin.

"Don't stare at him," Hugo said, interrupting my thoughts.

I focus back on the Master Keepers lining the Headquarter stairs. Sir Jasper steps out from the blood-red doors and draws everyone's attention forward. A breeze catches his dark emerald-embroidered Keeper's cloak and it billows like a windswept forest behind him. Right behind him, the Duke is there, too, ever coveting Sir Jasper's position as Head Keeper. I don't know how much longer Sir Jasper will live, but I hope he still has a lot of strength in him because having the Duke become Head Keeper would be unbearable. He already holds too many of the Keepers and contenders in the palm of his hand.

"Welcome everyone! On this September the 29th," Sir Jasper begins, "we celebrate our patron Michael the Archangel with our annual Keeper contender contests.

"As you all know, our people once knew how to survive well, despite the creatures. In fact, we thrived. We once had seven beautiful cities, all because we knew how to look out for each other and fight for each other. However, as our greed and selfish ambition grew, so did our vulnerabilities. The creatures turned us against each other and destroyed five of our cities. Today, they threaten the existence of the two that remain. This is why you contenders are called not merely to protect our people from our external threats, but also from the internal menaces of our own ignorance, thoughtlessness, and greed.

"In the spirit of Saint Michael, we strive to find contenders who distinguish themselves not only by their physical strength, tenacity, and intelligence, but also by their character and moral fortitude—humility, selflessness, compassion, integrity, and grace. To restore our people to who they once were, the cities need Keepers who can not only stand up to the creatures, but to corruption and greed as well. Each Keeper must be a beacon of light despite ever growing challenges."

As Sir Jasper says this, I can't help but think about my father, the sort of person Sir Jasper is warning against.

"So, without further ado, may the most worthy among you rise up, not just as the leaders of our guards and warriors, but as steadfast defenders of all that is right and good."

As everyone applauds, Sir Jasper pulls open the roll of contenders who have been selected to advance to the final

Keeper contest. The courtyard stills. While some will walk through the doors standing behind Sir Jasper, others of us will have to leave the Keeper Headquarters for good— maybe to become a guard instead of a Keeper. But we have all given our best for this.

I steal a glimpse at Colin again. His face is stern and cold like stone. His hair is like the weariest of midnights while his eyes are like the grayest of freezing rains. He seems incapable of joy.

"Molly," Hugo nudges me in the ribs and squeezes my hand. "Come on! He called your name."

He has? He called me first?

As I hug Hugo, I can't help but notice Colin from over my brother's shoulder. For the first time in five years, his eyes meet mine. Time seems to stagnate and everything else around me disappears.

I let go of my brother and lower the hood over my head. As I walk toward the Head Keeper, the courtyard's gravel crunches too loud under my boots. The Duke, his dark features striking, stands at the bottom of the steps, his eyes fixed on me. As I climb the steps, I avoid him.

As I stand there, Sir Jasper looks at me, his eyes taking me in from over both his list and ornate glasses. I clench my satchel in closer, focus on my boots, and the creases, lines, and scuffs in their leather.

"Miss Fitzpatrick," he says.

He is the only one who matters. He leads me in my vows, and when he finishes, declaring me an official Keeper contender, all I can think about is that I have the notebook. I wish Hugo had never given it to me, or that I could have at least returned it to him, pretending ignorance about it. But even just knowing its existence changed everything. Nothing can ever be the same. I have to do what's right.

I walk through the Headquarter doors, ready to hand the treasonous pages over as soon as the opportunity presents itself. Unfortunately, it will likely be my first and last act as a Keeper contender.

After our congratulatory speeches and costuming, we sit down for our first examination. Our essay question is: "To what extent were the Mirror of Sparrows' omniscient powers good for the cities of both Saint Michael and Saint Selaphiel?" Not my favorite topic.

The Mirror of Sparrows' omniscient powers were a definite curse. According to my history lessons, the Mirror exponentially increased political tensions within the cities, not to mention, caused my father to murder the Head Keeper and his wife. Of course, I won't include that in my essay.

I do argue that any object with that much power should be prohibited and destroyed, because it can only cause greed, contention, and abuse. No human can ever be trustworthy enough to handle such an object, and no one could ever resist its use for their own ambitions, not even the most benevolent of Keepers. Plus, even if the Mirror is used by a truly good person to protect the cities, knowledge is still not capacity. Just because the Mirror could point to where help is needed, that doesn't mean the Keepers could respond in practicality.

As I proofread my essay, the Duke enters the testing room. Everyone must have taken notice because we all sit up a little straighter.

Like a hungry predator on the hunt for its weak prey, the Master Keeper prowls between the classroom's stone columns and archways, past our writing tables, searching for someone to devour. Why does it feel like the weak prey here will end up being me?

Though I try my best to focus on my quill, blotting paper, and writing, I have great difficulty concentrating. I glance toward my satchel. It still holds the notebook. I should have given it to Sir Jasper by now. Why haven't I?

I tuck a stray wisp of chestnut hair behind my ear and sneak a nervous glance at Colin—I'm not sure why. In that same moment, Colin eyes me, too. He is impossible for me to read, but we lock eyes for the second time today.

Out of nowhere, the Duke appears beside me and lashes his sword on my desk. I almost fall off my chair, my ink-pot rocks, and the black liquid splatters everywhere.

"Are you more interested in gawking at the male contenders or in becoming Keeper?" he asks.

I feel myself blush with shame. What am I supposed to do? I try to lift my essay out of the ink, but the Duke drives me back, the sharp edge of his sword now pushing into my shoulder. My hand shoves the weapon away, slicing my skin. My hand is bleeding.

"Stay where you belong," he tells me, pushing me back down with his gloved hand.

The ink is spreading and dripping over the edge of my desk. It pours onto me, the stone floor, and my satchel. The notebook is going to be stained and ruined. With the tip of my foot, I try to nudge the bag out of the flow, but I miscalculate. Its balance is thrown off. As the bag topples over, everything in it comes tumbling out. Worst of all, my father's notebook falls onto the floor, on display for everyone to see.

The Duke does a double take, his forehead creases. Time pauses, except his eyes glimmer. His entire demeanor shifts. I can't quite breathe. He must somehow know what it is, and he wants it. He pulls my chin up with his gloved fingers—I have no choice but to look at him—and he leans in closer to me.

"As I'm sure you already know," he says as he picks up my contraband with the tip of his foot, "there are no written materials allowed in the testing room. Cheaters are disqualified from the Keeper contests. You are finished here. You must now leave."

When the Duke realizes what my notes really are, disqualification will be the least of my worries. I will be confirmed and condemned a traitor. Who knows what else will happen then?

"What is going on here?" Sir Jasper walks up to us, concern etched into his brow. I should have given him the notebook first thing.

The Duke's jaw juts out. "She's brought in written materials."

Sir Jasper reaches his hand toward me. Warmth emanates from his tired, baggy eyes, and the weathered but strong Head Keeper lifts me out of my mess. He notices my cut palm.

"There are rags and water in the servant's hall closet," he says.

"Yes. Clean up this mess," the Duke orders.

While I'm glad to ease away from my chair, the predator still has my father's notebook.

I walk past the other contenders, all are pretending to work on their essays, except for Hugo, who looks up at me. I've never seen my brother so pale, and his fists are tight and balled up. He really messed this day up, but my heart squeezes with the knowledge that I had planned to turn him in. I was so upset, but he's my family. Even when we had nobody else, we've always been there for each other. I hate that no matter what I do, it feels wrong.

In the hallway, once I am alone, I try to pull myself together, but tears still come. Everything has gone for the worst.

After I wipe my face, I check my wound—not too deep, but I will need to bandage it. Then, I wash my hands out, and find the cleaning supplies. I fill a wooden bucket with water and grab several rags.

Though I make my way back to the testing room, I am too ashamed to return in. I'm no longer a contender—just a traitor's daughter and a failure who must clean up the terrible mess she's made. My stained fingers squeeze one of the rags, and through the narrow crack between the door and the wall, I watch the remaining contenders finish handing in their essays.

After Sir Jasper dismisses everyone, Hugo walks toward my hiding place. He opens the door and slips in next to me and gives me a big hug.

"Now that the Duke has the notebook, the Keepers will think I've been hiding the Mirror this whole time," I say.

"We're not actually sure what information the notebook contains," Hugo says. "If anything, the instructions are less than obvious. I've been studying dad's notes for the last five years, ever since he gave it to me, and haven't been able to figure anything out. I doubt the Keepers will have any idea what the book is about. They can't accuse us of anything. The clues on how to find the Mirror of Sparrows are in there, though. They are just well hidden."

I don't know what to tell him. He's talking fast, doing his best at being reassuring, but it all feels meaningless.

"Did you hear me, Molly? There is no real evidence in there against you."

"So maybe they won't condemn me for treason, and it's only my dream of becoming a Keeper that is gone."

"I'm sorry all this happened. I just thought it was a fitting occasion to finally share the notebook with you. I had been trying to protect you by not showing it to you, but I realize I messed up. But I'm going to help you untangle this mess. I promise."

"At this point, I don't think too much can be done."

With one hand, Hugo takes the bucket from me, and with the other, my bleeding hand. "The Duke is gone now. Let's go back in there. I'll help you."

Together, we return to the testing room. At my seat, the notebook is gone and only an inky muddle remains. We kneel on the ground, and Hugo helps me scrub the desk, floor, and chair.

"I never should have sprung the notebook on you," he says.

I nod. I appreciate his sincerity and new understanding of the predicament he put me in.

"I'm going to try to talk to Sir Jasper," I tell him. "Maybe he can still help us."

"What are you going to tell him?" he asks.

"I don't know yet." All I know is I have to do something.

"Do whatever you think is best. I trust you."

After we finish cleaning, he leaves. I am alone with Sir Jasper. He is sitting at a big table and has started reading the essays.

CHAPTER 5
Colin

I still can't believe Sir Jasper selected me. In the hallway, the glow of candlelight illuminates the stone arches that frame my way toward the exit. I hurry forward, pulling my hood low over my eyes and push past the other contenders as fast as I can. My head is pounding from the Remedy withdrawals, and there is not much more of this I can take. I need to go away before anyone tries to talk to me, and I especially don't want to see the Duke.

Once through the gates, I disappear into the quietness of night, and at long last, everything is silent, and I'm alone. As I cross the iron bridge that will lead me home, I wish I could be more like this structure: strong, purposeful, true. The bridge keeps its passersby safe from the River Trent's raging waters below. I pause, taking time to admire the craftsmanship as well as the river. It's engorged by the day's rains.

I kick a pebble over the edge and watch it plummet into the torrents that thunder beneath. They engulf the stone before it can even touch the waters.

I lean my elbows onto the cold rail and push my head into my hands, trying to bring order to the chaos engulfing my thoughts. *Sir Jasper selected me.* He said he accepted me because I tried to take care of that woman in the forest. I can hardly believe it.

I'm not sure how long I have been standing here, but I sense someone else on the bridge, lingering. My pulse quickens. When I look, Hugo is there. Besides the Duke, he's the last person I want to see. He seems like he wouldn't hesitate to follow in his father's footsteps.

"Good thing the Ruler and the Duke were there to make sure you didn't lose face today," he says.

His words sting, and I can't see his features, but imagine him smirking at me. I turn away, but he steps in right behind me.

"I wouldn't come near me if I were you," I tell him as I try to unclench my fists. My heart is racing, and my whole body feels full of fire. Why is Hugo even here?

Hugo laughs. "You may think you're Keeper material, but I'll tell you what everyone knows you are," he continues. "The Duke's little puppet."

He reaches for my shoulder, but the instant his fingers make contact, I grab and twist his arm, forcing him away. His eyes hold mine, and everything in me despises him. "It's about time you faced the truth," he says. "You're a sad peon for that monster."

I twist harder, pushing him back.

"You walk around like the world owes you something." He leans in. "If only the father you claim to care so much about could see you now."

"He would be here if your father hadn't killed him," I say, and before I even realize what I'm doing, I swing my fist around, straight into his face. His nose gushes red, and he staggers back, disoriented, but continues—his grin broadening through the blood. He keeps coming toward me, bloody face and all. "Don't get me wrong," he says. "I was glad you made the Keeper contests today. Now we can really find out what you are made of. But I highly doubt you will last."

I barrel toward him, my shoulder landing in his stomach. The full weight of my body crashes into him, and Hugo doubles over.

"You're pitiful," he shouts as he recovers. "The only person you care about in this city is yourself."

I shove him against the rail of the bridge and keep pushing. I don't want to hear anymore. Because of the rain, Hugo slips on the slick ground and loses his footing, tumbling backward and teetering on the edge of the bridge's rail, right over the water. He barely manages to grab hold of one of the metal bars to keep from falling into the river. His knuckles, strained with desperate tension, are all I can focus on, but I know he's screaming.

"Pull me up!" he shouts.

Dangling over the torrential waters, Hugo's eyes are wide with fear.

Shaking from shock, I reach for him and wrap my hands around his forearms to hoist him to safety. When Hugo lands back onto the bridge, he holds on to one if the beams, trying to catch his breath. When he stands up, his face and clothes all bloody and bitter fury is flaring up across his face.

"The Keepers are going to find out about this," he says. "Sir Jasper'll see you're disqualified for good, no matter who your mentor or father is."

He was the one who provoked me, but I don't want to continue. I'm sure Hugo will make good on his promise and see to it that everyone finds out about this, and I just forfeited my last chance at Keeper selection. How could I be that easily baited and allow my anger get the best of me? I just lost everything, again. It all happened so fast.

As Hugo disappears into the streets at the other end of the bridge, I sink down to the ground, head pressed against the rail of the bridge. The thing is, what scares me most is that much of what Hugo said might be right.

Am I the Duke's puppet? What would my father say? Maybe I never did deserve to be Keeper.

Chapter 6
Molly

I'm not sure how to approach him. I don't know what to say to the wizened Head Keeper or how to interrupt his concentrated work. Sir Jasper continues to sit at the monumental table at the front of the room, reading through the contender essays. I can only see the top of his creased and wrinkled brow because his attention is on the papers. His gray hair is pulled back in a tight and smooth ponytail. For his age, he has broad, strong shoulders. With his quill, he keeps jotting down notes on all the work. I wonder what he is writing and what his thoughts are on the question we all just wrote about. It amazes me how he takes the time to be involved in each contender's endeavor to become Keeper.

I put away the cleaning supplies and gather my belongings, whatever is left of them, and my destroyed essay—I don't have the heart to throw it out. Then, like a mouse that wants to ask a lion for mercy, I tip-toe to Sir Jasper's big table. I know he's the only one who might be able to help me, but I also know I don't deserve his help. It's horrible to have disappointed him like this after everything he has meant to Hugo and me.

Behind him hang the portraits of the most famous past Keepers and Rulers, including Colin's father. It's like they're all staring at me, and that each one of them knows I'm here, except for Sir Jasper.

I clear my throat.

Sir Jasper sets down the papers and raises his eyes to meet mine. Though he is serious and even a bit stern, the Head Keeper is not condescending. His eyes shine with an earnest curiosity about what I might have to say and why I'm still here. He slides on his mysterious, famous glasses—everyone wonders about the renowned bifocals of the old Keeper. I've never seen them this up-close before, but now, I can't help but be mesmerized by their elaborate emerald-encrusted rims.

"Well," Sir Jasper says. "What do you have to say?"

"I didn't cheat," I say. "I promise."

"But didn't you bring written materials into the testing room?" he asks. "You know that's against the rules."

I wish I could explain to him that the rule in question was the last issue on my mind, and that I had to bring in the notebook because I was planning on turning it in—because I didn't want to be a traitor and because the future of the Keepers might depend on it—but I was scared and worried about Hugo. It never occurred to me I was breaking a rule.

In thoughtful quietness, Sir Jasper continues to appraise me.

"Miss Fitzpatrick," he starts up again. "As you are well aware, I care about you and your brother very much.

Nevertheless, you must abide by the rules, even if you do have much on your mind."

I lower my head. "I must have been a tremendous disappointment to you after all the trouble you have been through for me."

"You were never trouble. When everything happened with your parents, you were mere children, precious in every way, and I am a Keeper, after all, aren't I? That's my job. But now, back to the rules and the contest: what bothers me just as much as that mysterious notebook is that, during the test, you showed yourself so prone to intimidation and anxiety. A true Keeper cannot give into these—even under the most difficult of circumstances. You must keep your wits about you and not be so easily unwound."

I feel myself blushing. He's right, though. I should keep my wits about me.

He examines me through his fancy spectacles a few moments longer, his thick gray eyebrows furrowed. Then, he hands me some blank sheets of paper.

"Now, if you have a better grasp of the commitment you are making, the commitment to keep your attention focused on your objectives and to follow the rules, you may rewrite an abbreviated essay while I finish reading these. You're still in a whole lot of hot water, and you only have until I leave, but try your best."

"Thank you," I say, taking the paper.

I sit down at the nearest desk, pull out my quill, ink, and blotting sheet, and I write with all my might, even if just to show Sir Jasper he hasn't wasted his time on me. Everything except for my opinions about the Mirror—the notebook, Colin, the Duke, Sir Jasper, everyone and everything—I push out of my mind. I need to focus. And I do. The world around me disappears, and words pour out of me as fast and thoughtful as they ever have.

"Are you finished?"

I have no idea how much time has elapsed by the time Sir Jasper speaks to me, but my fingers are sore, and I have written almost the whole essay. I only need a few concluding sentences. I don't make him wait, however, and bring him what I have. He skims over my work, then sets it down.

"Good-night, Miss Fitzpatrick," he says. "I wish you and your brother all the best in your fights tomorrow."

I bow my head in thanks. "I hope that, some day, I can pay you back for your kindness."

He smiles. "That's not necessary. Your continued strength and persistence are what I'd rather have."

After, I wrap my cloak around me and tread through the training hall toward the doors, back out to the rest of the world. I wonder whether the Duke might still be here, somewhere. I shouldn't worry, but as I walk through the empty stone hallway, the silence seems to hold some sort of trap.

When I find myself beyond the iron gates, I realize my fears were unfounded—like Sir Jasper said, I need to keep my wits about me. I take a few deep breaths. Colin, the Duke, the ink, and the notebook are, for just a moment, in a world apart.

At the Straight Street Bridge, all I hear is the roar of the river below me. In this moment, everything going wrong is distant. I savor the gratitude I have for Sir Jasper, and for this glimpse at the captivating world that lies beyond our city walls.

As I meander home, the empty cobblestone streets are blurs of heavy rain and shadows. I begin again to process everything that happened—especially my shameful predicament. Everyone thinks I'm a cheater, that I never deserved to be competing in the first place, and now even more so. Not to mention, the Duke has the notebook. It's almost too much for me to handle. Though Sir Jasper is giving me another chance, I'm concerned I will bring him further shame. How can I possibly keep my wits about me?

Having trudged my whole way home through the rain, I at long last arrive at my front door. Judging from the darkness up the narrow steps, Hugo hasn't returned home yet. I light a lantern, pull off my wet boots, and flop on the ground at the bottom of my bed. I wish I could just sit here, but it's cold. Plus, my hand is throbbing.

I hang my wet clothes and start a fire in the stove, with a kettle of water on top for tea. As the water boils, the steam rises and warmth fills the room. There is so much to think about, but the coziness of home and the rain's rhythm on the roof are soothing. I pull out a cup, open a tin of dried mint leaves, and take from it what I need. While the tea brews, I clean the cut on my hand and bandage it, then wrap myself in a warm blanket.

Drinking in a long sip of the peppermint honey deliciousness, I close my eyes and allow my shoulders to relax. It's been a very long day. Just as my thoughts steady, the trap door flies open. Hugo barges in, his face drenched with rain and smeared with blood, not to mention swollen and changing color. When he hangs his cloak, I see the new sweater I made him is bloodied and torn as well.

"What happened?" I ask, rising to my feet.

"Colin almost threw me off the Straight Street Bridge," he says, pacing. "But he'll be disqualified when the Masters find out. He has no business being a Keeper. No one training under the Duke should ever be allowed to qualify."

I haven't seen my brother this angry in a long time. He's boiling and whistling like an overheated kettle.

"Why were you two even together?"

"I don't know, really. I was on my way home when I saw him staring out at nothing, over the bridge. He seemed off. When he saw me, everything spiraled. I don't even know what happened. That guy has serious anger issues. I've been walking around ever since—what with the notebook and everything—I'm trying to pull my thoughts together. Unlike everyone else, I'm not going to let him believe he's above consequences."

After today, I'm in no position to judge anyone, so I stay silent.

Hugo sits down beside the stove, warming his hands.

"Do you want a cup of tea?" I ask while already making him one.

"That would be great. How did it go with Sir Jasper?"

"He's given me another chance to compete," I tell him as I pour extra honey into his cup and hand it to him. "He let me rewrite the essay and wished me luck on tomorrow's fights."

"That's great." Taking a sip of the tea, he considers me. "I'm glad that worked out. What did you say?"

I begin preparing a basin with cool and hot water for him, so he can clean himself. "Honestly, not much," I say. "Mostly, I just apologized." But I sigh. "Except I doubt anyone wants me there, especially now."

"Who cares what other people think? No one wants me there either, but you don't see me worried about it. Just focus on winning your fights."

I realize the truth in what he's saying, but it's not realistic for me to not care about what other people think. The bottom line is, I do care. I'm not like Hugo.

When I plop myself down beside him, he wraps his arms around me and gives me a hug, holding me a few moments.

"It's going to work out," he says. "Now, we just need to sort out the notebook situation."

"If you don't mind my asking, why did you choose to give me the notebook today?" I don't like to blame him after what he just went through, but it does seem like a reasonable question. I know my brother wouldn't intentionally harm me, but his nonsensical decision still hurt.

"I've been trying to figure out the instructions in it for years." His voice lowers. "I had hoped you might see something in there I hadn't, and that we might finally break free from our endless rut. And then, it seemed like the perfect gift for the Keeper contender celebration. I'm sorry I misjudged the situation." His eyes fix onto mine, sharp. "Anyway, I have a plan. I wasn't so sure about it before, but now I see it is the only way. We need to retrieve it before anyone figures out what it is."

"What plan?" I have a big knot tightening in my stomach over this sudden new idea of his.

He stands and grabs his cloak. "Don't worry. It's better for you not to ask me, but you can probably figure it out. How many people do you think can help us with the notebook?"

"I can't think of any."

"Try harder." My brother's face brightens up with a big smile, as he backs up his way to the door.

I try to stop him. "You are worth more to me than any notebook or secret it contains. Whatever you are planning, it cannot end well. I'm scared something will happen to you, Hugo."

"We have no choice. I have to try something. Just stay calm and keep your wits about you."

I'm tired of people saying that.

"A least let me help," I say.

"The best way you can help us is to have a decent night sleep and to do well in your fights tomorrow."

Before I can contain him, he's down the stairs. I want to pick up my cloak and run after him, but he has made his choice. I don't think there is anything I can say or do to sway him, so I have to let him go.

As I kneel down to pray, the wood is hard and cold under me, but the sound of the rain's thundering downpour is comforting. I pray that, just like this storm is enveloping this city, angels would protect Hugo and his plan, however wild and crazy they might both be.

CHAPTER 7
Colin

The shop bells jingle several times.

"Can you check who it is?" Uncle Felix calls out.

No, I want to say. After what just happened, I don't want to see anyone. But this is Uncle Felix asking, so I do it.

When I open up, there stands none other than Hugo, and he's a bloody mess. My shoulders instantly roll back. Does he want another fight?

I don't want Uncle Felix to see him, so I step out of the shop, shutting the door behind me. I focus my sights down the windy alleyway, trying not to lose my temper a second time tonight.

"Why are you here?" I ask.

"Molly didn't cheat today," he says. "And it isn't fair that she would be disqualified for something she didn't do. It's not fair that you can be such a screw-up and make it, while she does everything in the best way possible and still not make it. I need you to help me get her notebook back and prove her innocence to the other Master Keepers."

I laugh. "Then she shouldn't have brought the book in. That was her mistake."

Hugo leans in close to me, his eyes like fire. I want to shove him away.

"Unless you help me retrieve her notebook from the Duke," he says, "the Keepers are going to find out about what happened on that bridge. But if you help me, your secret will forever be safe."

"No one will care about what you have to say," I tell him.

"Not every Keeper is the Duke's pawn, and since a notebook was enough to do one contender in, think about what almost killing someone will do."

It is true that I've disgraced myself in front of the Keepers enough as it is, but I can't go after this notebook.

"If you step back into that house and decide not to help me, I will go to the Keepers right now, and everyone will find out about what you did." His features are set, full of unflinching determination.

"This is the Duke we're talking about, remember?" I say. "It will make everything way worse for Molly if he finds out the notebook is missing." Realistically though, my guess is the Duke probably left Molly's notebook in a corner of his office to collect dust and won't notice if it's gone. If he does eventually realize it's missing, he might blame it on the carelessness of a servant.

"The Duke doesn't deserve your loyalty. What matters is that you have nothing to lose and everything to gain by helping me. You know how to get into the Duke's mansion, right?"

I've pretty much grown up there. I know the mansion inside out, but this is a bad gamble. I don't trust Hugo, but on the other hand, I can't let him tell everyone what I've done. And it's not my loyalty to the Duke I'm worried about. It's being caught.

"How do I know you'll keep quiet about the bridge?" I ask.

"I swear to you, on my life." Hugo actually places his right hand over his heart. "And should anything go wrong, I will take the full blame for it."

I wish there was another way, but I really can't let anything further jeopardize me becoming a Keeper.

"Wait here," I tell him. "I need my tools."

Hugo and I hustle through the labyrinth of alleyways to the other side of the city and into the back gardens of the Duke's mansion.

"I go alone from here," I say.

Hugo laughs. "Together, or nothing at all."

My hands ball up. This guy's audacity knows no bounds, yet what choice do I have? So I take Hugo to the secret tunnel I know will lead inside. The Duke showed me this passage after my father died. I guess it was his way of making me feel at home.

We duck behind a large bush and into pitch black darkness. Except for the sound of our breathing and the occasional rodent scratching away from us, Hugo and I move ahead in silence. The smell of cold, wet earth permeates the air, and I close my eyes and let my fingers pull along the dirt walls. Familiar stones and roots protrude through the edges, the moisture cooling my hands.

"These walls look like they could crumble in on us any moment now," Hugo says.

"They won't," I tell him.

When we come to the end of the tunnel, I press my ear to the door leading inside. The sound resonates well through it, and I can tell the Duke's guards are walking past.

"What are we waiting for?" Hugo asks.

"Guards," I tell him.

Hugo laughs. "The Duke has guards in his own home?"

"Apparently for good reason," I say and pull my hood up.

Once the hallway sounds empty, I push the door open into the back of a fake armoire. When Hugo and I have fully entered the large space that is the Duke's mansion, Hugo pauses. The red marble floors, the high vaulted ceilings, the massive painted portraits, the chandeliers, the mirrors, drapes, gold plated furniture; an endless excess. I've gotten used to it all, but to someone like Hugo, it must be more than anything he could have imagined.

"Is this for real?" he asks. "How can he live like this when the rest of us are barely scraping by?"

I can't contest that this is undeniably excessive for any one person. I never questioned it all, but now I do.

"We need to keep moving," I say.

I take Hugo down several corridors and push through a carved door on the side of a fireplace. Next, I lead Hugo down a long, oak-paneled passage. We hustle ahead until we make it outside the Duke's office. Our secret entryway is disguised behind the wooden walls and not visible from within the office.

I put my eye to the keyhole. The Duke's hundreds of books line the walls, as well as maps of all the former Seven Cities and the wilderness in between. There are remnants of a fire still glowing in the fireplace, in front of which are a big chair and his huge desk. Opposite from where Hugo and I are concealed is the official entrance—shut, as I had hoped.

"We're good to go. I hope we can find that notebook you're looking for."

When we enter the office, the familiar smell of the cloves and tobacco the Duke uses permeates the air. It causes me to pause, but I snap out of it and head straight for the desk. A small dog with long black and brown hair and little ears runs out from the other side of it: Nolan. Why would the Duke leave him here, alone in the dark?

Nolan knows me but not Hugo, and he growls and yaps at him.

"Sit," I order Nolan. Good thing he's an obedient dog. While I watch him, Hugo goes to search around the office.

"I can't find it," he says. "Are you sure he would keep it here?"

"Unless he threw it out," I say.

"I doubt that," Hugo answers.

"Check inside the desk then," I tell him.

Hugo attempts to force the drawers open. "It's locked."

I come round to where Hugo is and examine the lock. Not too hard to pick, but under the circumstances—what with the dark, Nolan, and the probability of guards showing up at any second—it could be challenging. But that's what I brought my tools for, just in case.

"Can we get in there?" Hugo asks. His voice is tense with desperation.

"Most likely," I tell him. I wipe my hands down and pull my lock-picking tools out from my pocket. I select three and slide them into the lock. It is impossible to see, but I can figure out what's going on well enough. *Click.* I pull the desk compartments open and fumble inside. There's the notebook.

I hand it to Hugo, who lets out a sigh of relief and looks like he could hug me.

But why did the Duke lock that notebook up? And could he have left Nolan here to guard it? I can't help but wonder what the big deal about this notebook is.

As I shut the drawer, Nolan starts to bark again, and a voice comes from behind the main door.

"Who's in there?" the person demands. A guard.

Time to run.

Hugo places the notebook in my hands. "Give it to Molly," he tells me. "No matter what."

I don't understand. "What are you talking about? Let's go." Why isn't he coming with me?

Several people talk outside while a key turns in the lock.

I try to grab his arm, but he pushes my hand away.

"This is the only way. We can't both escape. We won't make it. I need to hold the door. Besides, didn't I tell you I'd take the blame? You just give that notebook to Molly—tomorrow morning, at the fights." He runs to the door to hold the guards back.

"But the notebook? They'll know it's missing."

"I'm going to say I burned it in the fire." He smirks like this situation is nothing, but by the tightness in his jaw and the intensity in his eyes, this is everything.

Time is out. The guards are pushing the door open, so I scramble back into the passageway, shutting Hugo and the secret door behind me, before anyone discovers I was there.

CHAPTER 8
Colin

As I sprint back through the Duke's secret passageways, I struggle to make sense of Hugo's decisions. Is he going to tell them I was there? And if not, why would he sacrifice himself for the sake of this journal? Why is it so important?

Once back outside the tunnel, I peer through the branches and foliage into the Duke's immaculate landscaping, searching for signs of movement. The guards have not sounded the alarm or come out yet—a sign that Hugo's plan might be working. I secure the journal under my cloak and scale the garden wall. Thankfully, the neighboring street is empty, and I don't think anyone has seen me. I dust off the stray leaves and dirt and move on.

When I make it back to the shop, Uncle Felix is still awake, sitting in his big leather chair and reading a newspaper by the light of a single candle.

"Where were you?" Uncle Felix's voice is shaking a little. It seems the progress I made with the lockbox is already coming undone.

"I was out with some friends," I tell him.

"I saw you leave with Hugo Fitzpatrick. Since when have you had him as a friend?"

I have no good answer, and I can't look at my uncle. The last thing I want him to know is that, after everything that happened outside the walls, I almost killed Hugo, then broke into the Duke's mansion in order to not lose my spot in the contests.

We wait in awkward silence, until he mercifully changes the subject. Holding his candle up so its light shines on my face, he says, "I should mention, Sir Jasper came by for you, too."

Why would the Head Keeper come here? Could he have found out about the bridge?

"I showed him the box you made, and he examined it for a long time."

"Why did you show it to him?" My words come out harsher than I intended, but I don't mean to sound antagonistic. I'm just confused and tired.

"Because I am proud of you and wanted him to know what you are capable of—especially after he told me he great news."

I shake my head, almost embarrassed.

"Do you know what he said?" Uncle Felix continues, and he doesn't give me the chance to answer. "He said that despite what happened with the Remedy, you showed true courage and compassion out there. He said your actions in the wilderness showed the Keeper in you that he's been hoping to see, and that you have incredible potential."

"He said that?" I'm stunned. It's the last thing I thought I would hear.

"He sure did. And he told me about your essay, too. He said you wrote that people are the ones who make a true difference, not objects—he also mentioned you listed me and also the Fitzpatrick girl as examples."

I stand there, exposed and raw.

"Thank you, Colin. Now, what's this about Molly? You never even usually eat the bread she brings. What's going on?"

"I don't know." I shake my head. "I really don't want to talk about it, and I need to sleep."

Uncle Felix sighs and sets his candle down. "There's one more thing I need to tell you before you go upstairs. It's important, otherwise I wouldn't keep you." He adjusts himself forward in his chair. "Sir Jasper explained to me that you are too young for the Remedy—all new Keepers are. It's too dangerous. That wasn't the reason it didn't work on you, though. He explained that for people with deep sorrow, a regular dose is not enough to face the creatures."

"How can I ever become a Keeper then?" I snap.

"Sir Jasper says you can. You have to fight with fire and work on healing from your sorrow. And the Head Keeper also took the time to remind me that neither he nor your father ever used Remedy."

I can't help but laugh.

My uncle folds his hands together on his lap. "I think he's right. Sir Jasper says he can help you, but you have to trust him."

"Doesn't he realize he's part of my problem?" My words come out bitter, and I start up the stairs, almost stumbling in my avalanche of anger. I expect Uncle Felix to stop me, but he doesn't. I enter my room and throw off my cloak and boots. I light the few candle remnants I have—I don't want to go back downstairs for fresh ones—

and collapse on my bed, peeling off my sweaty socks and stretching my legs out.

After a few moments of quiet, I remember I have the journal and need to figure out its significance. Within its leather binding are pages upon pages of handwritten notes and drawings. The rocky cursive is in brown ink and framed with detailed illustrations. I can't make out any clear author, and from what I can tell, it doesn't seem to contain anything Molly could have used to cheat with. So why did she have it with her?

The dates go back to both before and after my parents died. As I skim through the first pages, I realize the writer must have been a Keeper—maybe even a Master Keeper—because of the details in many of the entries are about Keeper trainings. On the last page, I see the initials M.F. Could the F be for Fitzpatrick? What was their father's first name? I can't remember—it was different—but the point is, could this journal have belonged to Molly and Hugo's father? My mouth tastes like bile, and I set the book on the worktable. Though I've had enough to think about for one day, I can't help but wonder why the Duke had the notebook locked up and guarded.

On the way to the arena, I clutch the journal tightly under my cloak. The crowds are out. Not only must they be excited to witness the combat portions of the testing, but also for the awaited influx of fresh provisions. People swarm through the celebration market buying foods, crafts, trinkets, and every random knickknack imaginable. Normally, I would like this and all the clever contraptions, but right now, the chaos grates against my nerves. I pull my hood low and navigate through the marketers.

According to Hugo, Molly should still be fighting this morning, despite what happened yesterday.

A guard stops me at the contenders' entrance to the arena. By the formal way in which he holds himself, this man takes his job seriously.

"Restricted area," he says. "Read the sign."

I push my hood back. Though contenders aren't supposed to arrive until before their fights, I'm hoping he'll make an exception.

He blushes. "Colin Kelly. I should have known, but I wasn't expecting you to arrive this early since it's the girls' fights this morning. I'm very sorry, but your changing room isn't available yet."

"It's not about that. I need to talk to someone," I say. "It's urgent." The sooner she has the notebook, the sooner I will be assured no one will know what happened on the bridge last night.

He shakes his head no. Apparently this guy is a stickler for the rules. Doesn't he realize who I am?

"I need to speak with Molly Fitzpatrick," I say. Surely he knows the weight that name carries for me. Everyone does.

His forehead creases with confusion. "We all agree she shouldn't be here," he says. "But I still can't let you in to see her—not before her fight."

"It's not what you think," I say. "I need to correct a misunderstanding before our competitions today. With our family history and everything, I know that doesn't make sense, but to be a good Keeper, I have to do this. I'm under strict orders."

"Rules are rules," he says, waving his pointer finger at me. I'm tempted to smash it off. I hadn't expected this to be the difficult part of the morning. "They are not to be broken under any circumstances."

"Listen," I say, taking several steps toward him. "The Duke was supposed to let you know. It's part of my mandatory penance for what happened the other day. You have to believe me because my chances of becoming a Keeper depend on this. You know what I did the other day, don't you?"

He shifts awkwardly. Obviously, he's heard about what happened. Apparently, everyone has.

"If you help me, I will make sure the Duke hears about it. But if you don't, he'll hear about that too." People fear the Duke, and I realize now, I have become accustomed to using his name like a weapon. From the guard's paling face, I know he fears him as well.

"I guess if the Duke told you...," the guard says, pointing me to a wall within the restricted area. "The room assignments are posted over there. Most people are not expecting her on the schedule, as you likely well know. It's a bit controversial."

"Thank you," I say and walk in to find Molly on the listings.

"I hope you do put in a good word for me," he continues.

I nod and then hurry down the passageway to find her preparation room, in case the guard changes his mind. I can't believe I'm doing this, running errands for the Fitzpatricks. Molly's room is directly below the huge wood bleachers, and the gathered crowd is already loud. The sound reminds me of how many people are following everything we are doing, and I wonder how many of them will know about me failing outside the walls.

I knock on Molly's door and wait. Today will be the first time I've spoken to her since we were small.

"Hugo?" she asks as she swings the door open.

"No. It's Colin," I say. "I do have something from Hugo, though."

She freezes, obviously shocked to see me here instead of her brother. Sparkles shimmer over most of her face, so it would be hard to tell, were it not for her widened brown eyes. An array of silver-blue strands wrap all around her, framing her. All contenders are outfitted with costumes, a necessary part of the show and tradition, and I hate to admit, but she looks striking in hers.

"Can I come in?" I ask.

She hesitates, but allows me past her. When she shuts the door behind herself, we are alone together. I hadn't pictured this as part of our exchange, but maybe this is good. When I wrote about her in my essay yesterday, I had been thinking about her secret bread deliveries and how she had tried her best to make things right by me and Uncle Felix. To my uncle, she had brought peace, but to me, only further anger—but I want to have more peace now, like Uncle Felix. Maybe this is my opportunity to try.

"You said you have something for me?" she says.

"I do." I pull the notebook from my cloak. "Just keep your side of the deal and don't say anything to anyone about what happened last night."

When I hand her the notebook, I can't help but notice our fingers almost brush. She opens the book and meanders through some of its pages, as if to check it really is her missing journal.

"Was it your father's?" I ask her. When our eyes meet, her strained look is enough for me to know the answer to my question is yes.

"How did you find it?" she asks me. "And where is Hugo?"

Thankfully, I don't have the time to answer her because someone outside her changing room knocks on the door. "It's time," they say.

"I'll be right there," she answers back, hiding the journal away in her belongings.

"Wait." As I turn to exit, she grabs hold of one of my arms. My eyes dart down to where her fingers are latched on to me. She must realize she has overstepped a boundary because she releases her grip right away.

"What?" I ask.

"Almost time for your fight," the voice shouts again through the door.

"Thank you," she says, her eyes fixed on mine. "Thank you for bringing me the notebook."

At that she is gone, and I am left alone in her changing room. I know I should leave, too, but I find myself lingering—caught off guard by everything that just happened.

Chapter 9
Molly

As the drums pound and call everyone to attention, I check my fighting stick and adjust the bandage around my hand. Where the Duke's blade cut me, my skin is still raw and painful. I take in the arena through an opening in the curtains. Even though it's only the first fight, a pretty large crowd has gathered. Their cheers fill the air as the Pit Master arrives, and my heart pounds in a mix of awe and fear. Everything is decorated in crimson like yesterday, but with added purple. The Pit Master's purple and red robe matches the decor, as well as his oversized, fancy feathered hat.

Set apart from the rest of the stands, Sir Jasper and his Master Keepers sit in a long, wooden box. The Ruler has joined them, too, but I cannot see the Duke. I guess that's a positive.

My main concern, however, is that I still haven't seen or heard from Hugo—besides Colin bringing me the notebook. It doesn't make sense. I bite my lip and survey the stands one more time.

Colin has entered the stands, but sits on his own, not near any of the contenders or Keepers.

"Welcome! Welcome! To one and all, welcome!" the Pit Master's voice thunders. He smiles broadly, raises his arms up, and the crowd cheers. They love him. He is quite a character. "Today's fights will be judged by the Ruler herself, as well as our dear Master Keepers," he explains. "They will award each contender points based on their performance. These will be added to the contender's overall score. Keep in mind your cheering will count, too! Whoever you cheer the loudest for will receive bonus points."

The Pit Master motions me into the arena. "And now, without further ado, our fearsome first contestants!"

I walk onto the red dirt, hundreds of silver-blue ribbons fluttering behind me.

The Pit Master motions toward the opposite side of the arena, and the audience applauds as my competitor steps forward. This girl is from Saint Selaphiel, and I don't really know her. She's painted her face in gold and browns, and feathers cling over her whole body like she's an elegant bird-of-prey.

We stand a few paces apart and take each other in. Her eyes are confident and strong. The Pit Master rings his first bell.

I glance around the stands again. Still no Hugo.

The Pit Master rings the second bell. This is it, and the crowd hushes.

My opponent pulls out her fighting stick, and so do I.

We circle each other, golden plumes and silver hues twisting and swirling around us.

She attempts a side thrust into my body, but I avoid it. She comes after me again, but I whip around and thrust my stick into her. She doubles over.

The crowd doesn't cheer. Normally, with every successful hit, they cheer.

My opponent lifts her head and flies through the air, trying to smack me across the shoulder. I manage to side-step out of the way, and, sweeping my hands down the length of my fighting stick, fling myself around and flip backward, strands of azure cascading behind me. After I land, I advance toward her, and we battle back and forth. We seem pretty evenly matched, but then, out of nowhere, my rival strikes me across the cheek. The side of my face feels like it explodes. My vision blurs, and the arena spins around me.

That was against the rules, but the crowd is still cheering. Won't the Pit-Master call the illegal hit?

My opponent grips my costume with both hands, fingers like talons, and we are face to face.

"You don't belong here," she says.

I try to step back, disoriented and dizzy, but am unable to.

She hits my fighting stick, and it slips through my fingers, onto the dirt.

The Pit Master rings the third bell. The fight is done. I can't believe it. It all happened so fast. But why isn't the Pit Master saying anything?

Guards open the pit doors, ushering us out.

As I pass through the exit, Sir Jasper—with his beautiful, weathered features, powerful stature, and staggering presence—is there. He steps between me and the guards.

"I need to see you immediately after you are cleaned up. I'll be waiting," he says.

I nod at what sounds like my official notice of disqualification and hug my arms around myself, weaving my fingers through the fabric strands enveloping me.

Several guards escort me through the mob of spectators, and the crowd erupts with jeers as I pass by. I have never felt this humiliated and unwanted. Never have I had a whole crowd turn against me. Maybe it's better Hugo wasn't here. Except Colin is there too, lips pinched, and eyes unexpectedly soft and lingering. Why has his demeanor shifted toward me?

When I make it to the solitude of my preparation room, I unwind my sweat-saturated costume. In the mirror, I see the side of my face swelling. It's going to be black and blue and tender for a while. Between that and my hand, I'm really starting to look busted up.

At the basin, I wash my make-up off. The water, face paint, and sparkles run down my arms and into a messy soup. I clean myself up, but am struggling. My costume and clothes are falling everywhere. I cannot seem to put everything back into order. Plus, now I have to go see Sir Jasper.

After everything, how can I face him or the crowd out there? The truth is, right now and with Hugo missing, I'm too disappointed and unraveled to see anyone. Besides, if I'm out of the selection, he doesn't need to talk with me immediately.

There are two ways out of this place for me now: the door or the window. I think I should opt for the window. I pack my belongings, tucking that cursed but precious notebook in the cloak pocket over my chest, and I push open the windowpane. I stick my head out, and when the coast is clear, I crawl out.

With my hood lowered, I do what I do best and disappear into the crowded market. The main city square and festivities satisfy my desperate need for distraction. The second fight has started—I can hear it—but thankfully, the commotion of the buying and selling drowns out most of the spectators' shouts. The grounds are thick with colorful displays, merchant stands, food stalls, shoppers, and the smells of roasting foods. I buy a few plums, as well as a waffle and some sausage slices. I'm famished, and we haven't had access to some of these foods in a while.

As I'm taking a bite out of one of my juicy plums, someone grabs my arm. I almost elbow the person, but I recognize the wrinkly hand. Sir Jasper.

It's like he's everywhere. How has he found me? Actually, the better question is why did I think I could evade him? He isn't Head Keeper for nothing.

I gulp down the food I am chewing, and wipe the plum juice from my face.

"You found me," I say.

"It wasn't that hard. I saw you crawl out of your window." The Head Keeper's face is taut with irritation as he slides on his ornate glasses. "Why did you leave after I told you to find me? What are you doing?"

My hands are full of food, so to me, it is plainly obvious what I am doing.

I turn the plums over in my hand. "I'm sorry I didn't find you. I need to search for Hugo." I shouldn't lie to Sir Jasper, but in my defense, I'm not thinking straight. And anyway, it's not a *total* lie. I'm desperate to figure out where my brother is. If only Colin had given me more information, that would have been really helpful.

Sir Jasper's brow furrows. "You don't know where your brother is?"

That wasn't a follow-up question I expected.

"He didn't come to my fight," I say. "He wasn't in the arena, and as much as possible, we try never to miss each other's fights."

Sir Jasper directs me to continue walking down an aisle of merchant stalls with him. When we come to a booth where large streams of beautiful fabric are sold, he nudges me behind the stand. Normally, I would have thought the billowing multi-colored fabrics captivating. But at the center of them stands a very peeved-looking Head Keeper.

"When was the last time you saw him?"

"Last night. Why?"

"Late last night, guards captured him attempting to steal your father's notebook from the Duke's personal office."

My blood drains, and the market around suddenly seems like another arena. I press the notebook in closer to myself and try to wrap my mind around everything Sir Jasper is telling me. I don't know whether it's anger, anxiety, panic, or sadness, but something floods me, maybe all of it, all at the same time.

"It doesn't make much sense," Sir Jasper echoes my thoughts, looking at where I press the notebook against myself. Does he somehow know I have it? Still examining me through his fancy spectacles, he continues: "But the Duke's guards caught your brother red-handed."

"Where is he?"

"In the Duke's custody. He will be tried and very likely convicted. Someone who was with him—helping him—stole away with the notebook. You, of course, are the prime suspect," Sir Jasper continues. "Unfortunately, I need to take you in. Apparently, you are the only person who would have been with him."

"I wasn't," I say.

Would Colin have set me up? He must have been the one with Hugo last night. He seemed different the last few days, but was it all a trick? I was so sure there had been a shift between us. Was his return of the notebook only part of a vengeful trap? Now, if Sir Jasper finds the notebook on me, it will confirm everyone's suspicions. No one will ever believe it was Colin who was with Hugo.

Sir Jasper peers at me through his spectacles. "Interesting."

Can he read my mind with his special glasses? "So, you claim you were not with your brother last night at the Duke's mansion?"

"I wasn't. I promise. I had no idea what Hugo was up to."

Sir Jasper's graying eyebrows furrow again. "Do you have some sort of alibi? A way to prove that you were not with your brother?"

I shake my head no. "I was alone in my room."

"Since the Ruler is here," the Head Keeper continues, "I didn't want to cause unnecessary disruption and held off arresting you until after the fight. But now, I must bring you in. Molly, everything points to you, and the Duke will personally prosecute you. Not only is he accusing you of theft and breaking and entering, but also of treason."

"What treason?" The penalty for treason is death. "He can't do that." I squeeze the notebook more tightly to my chest.

"Apparently, there is more to this notebook than some of your study notes." Sir Jasper's face is grim. "And the Ruler is taking his side."

Are Hugo and I bound to suffer our father's fate? Have his sins caught up with us once and for all?

"But you know the truth. You know I'm not lying."

Sir Jasper sighs. Even if he suspects I wasn't the one who stole the notebook, all the evidence stacks against me, and apparently there is nothing he can do to help. I can only think of one last option: run. Will I be fast enough?

Sir Jasper, still examining me through his peculiar glasses, raises a gray brow. He's been raising them a lot at me today.

"If running is really what you want to do," he says—he obviously can read my thoughts with his glasses—"the guards will be after you. The Duke will relentlessly pursue you. And you will come across even more guilty than before."

I have to try. If they catch me, the result will be the same as if I go with Sir Jasper now. They will imprison me and charge me with theft and treason either way. But I can't face them yet. First, I have to help Hugo.

I take one of my uneaten plums and place it in Sir Jasper's hands. The moment the Head Keeper takes it, I bolt, sprinting past stalls and people as fast as I can. Sir Jasper doesn't chase me or call guards after me, but I will still run as far and fast as possible.

CHAPTER 10
Colin

On my way home, I can't stop questioning Molly's loss—not because of her fighting, but the illegal moves that went unchecked by the Pit Master. My thoughts are interrupted, however, when I notice a column of smoke rising from the rooftops. The closer I arrive home, the more the gray plume seems to rise from my street. Next thing I know, I'm running through the narrow alleys, but as I round the last corner, I am stopped by a crowd of people congregated around the shop.

Pushing my way through, I call for my uncle, desperate for information. The shop windows are smashed in, and the door splintered, completely broken down.

"There's guards in there," a neighbor says, his face contorted with worry as he points into the shop. "The Duke, too."

A cold sweat forms on my neck. "Why is the Duke here?"

"The guards were turning everything over, then someone says they saw the forge fire spread. We don't think they meant to do it, because the Duke was cursing them."

After I carefully clear the remains of the door, a wave of heat assails me. Smoke stings my eyes and throat, so I lift my shirt over the bottom half of my face. As I continue forward, the crunch of glass under my boots stops me in my tracks. Shards cover the floor everywhere. There is not much I hate more. The deepest of anxiety wracks over me, and I almost turn back—but from the back of the shop comes an anguished cry.

"Help," my uncle cries out, his voice so weak I can hardly believe it's him. I continue toward his call, navigating an obstacle course of rubble, glass, and smoke. Lying in the middle of the overturned furniture and a mess of thrown tools, I finally find my uncle, blood-soaked and wheezing. I cradle his head in my hands, resting it in my lap, pushing the hair, sweat, and shards off his face. He is still wearing the key I gave him yesterday morning—and clutching the box, too.

Uncle Felix gasps for breath. "He's looking for you. He's searching after a journal."

When my uncle's old leather chair catches on fire beside us, I realize time is running out and we need to leave.

"I'm going to pull you out." I grab my uncle under his shoulders. He weighs a ton, so I have to adjust my grip. The smoke stings my eyes, and I can't quite keep them open. When I stumble over something, I almost drop my uncle, but recover just in time.

The creaking of the stairs alerts me someone is coming down from the bedrooms, and from behind the curtain of smoke, my mentor's familiar silhouette emerges.

"I know you helped steal the notebook." His words are bitter. "You're the only one who could have known how to find it. Where is it?"

As he walks closer, the Duke's heels crush into the already broken glass. Do I tell him? I can't decide what to do.

Uncle Felix squeezes my arm.

"Protect the notebook," he mumbles.

I look up at the Duke. "Why did you do this?" I shout.

"You did this," the Duke says. "You betrayed me, Colin. Of all people, you should have known better."

Uncle Felix pulls my hand on to the lockbox and then tugs me near. I'm scared to take my eyes off the Duke, but when my uncle nudges me again, I come close. His skin is paler than I thought possible, and his breathing erratic. "Fill the box with family treasures for me," he says.

"Stay with me," I beg him.

But where his hand was holding me before, it now goes limp. I gently shake him and check his breathing, but there is only nothingness. I can't believe he was just talking to me and now he is not. I grip my uncle's limp hand, squeezing hard, as if that could somehow bring him back. How can this be real?

Through the growing fire, the Duke's voice assails me again. "You will bring the notebook back to me, or you will suffer the same fate as your uncle."

"I don't have it," I shout.

He turns away, and his silhouette disappears through the flames and rubble. I don't see the Duke anymore after that.

When I assess my surroundings, the smoke is thickening as flames consume the wooden structure of the shop. At any moment, all my uncle's hanging metal works will smash down. I never cared for them as much as I do now, and it is not the fire consuming my home I feel, but a scorching anger roaring inside me.

I press my face into Uncle Felix's chest, taking in the presence and feel of him one last time, then I unravel the key from around his neck and take the lockbox. I don't want to leave, but everything is falling apart. I crawl out the back of the shop and climb up to the neighboring garden rooftops. There, I pause to look at the keys hanging around my neck. I can't believe this is happening.

I turn back just in time to see the shop and our cherished home collapse. I don't know whom to be angrier at, myself or the Duke. If only I hadn't been so short tempered on the bridge; if only I hadn't given in to Hugo, none of this would have happened. And now Molly has the journal. My body tenses and I kick some of the tiles near me, so hard a number of them tumble down to the alley below.

I have lost everyone I loved, and the lockbox and the clothes on my back are all I have left. As I run my fingers along the keys, I wish I could have stayed with Uncle Felix a little bit longer. I wish I could hear his voice one more time. I want him to be here, with me.

I sit down on the roof and, using the keys, I unlock the box. After the mechanisms turn and open, I'm surprised to find what my uncle put in there: my lock picking and metal engraving tools, as well as a note. In a hurried handwriting, he wrote, "You are my treasure. That journal is important. Protect it." I trace my fingers over the words and wonder when he did this. It had to have been just this morning, after I left to find Molly.

I lean my back into the cool stone wall behind me, pressing my head into the roughness of the bricks, desperate for relief. I close my eyes to compose myself, but in my mind's eye, everything is still burning. Uncle Felix is lying on the floor of the shop, surrounded with blood and shards, and I can almost feel the heat and his weight in my arms. But then, my mind skips back in time to how I found my parents when they died. Our home had been eerily still. I'd checked in their bedroom, but no one was there. When I'd called for them, no one answered. The last place I went to look was my father's office. The door was ajar, but I still had knocked. Peering inside, my parents' bodies lay on the floor surrounded by shards of broken glass—just like Uncle Felix. That's when my world fell apart.

At the memory, my heart aches more than I can bear, and I force my eyes open. While the image of my parents is gone, my home and the lock shop are still collapsed, burning in front of me, all over that cursed notebook.

As I sit here, the loss pours like hot tar over me—burning, immobilizing, wretched. My body can't help but ache for the comfort and peace it had received from the Remedy.

The Remedy…

Though I hated its aftereffects, it had melted my fear away. It had given me enormous strength and confidence. I wish I could feel that way right now. Just a little bit of it might make all the difference. Maybe it could help me survive this. Right now, I need any help I can get in order to cope with this pain. Losing Uncle Felix is more than I can bear.

I fiddle with the keys and lockbox. I'm completely on my own now. I have no one.

Should I find some Remedy? The desire for how it made me feel is pulsing through me and is the only thing

I want; just to get me through this, until I figure something out.

A thick rain begins to fall, and it prompts me to get moving. I look one more time at the home Uncle Felix and I once had. After that, it's not difficult for me to figure out where to head to next. My feet practically take me there on their own. The Keeper Headquarters are where the Remedy is hidden, and I happen to know exactly where.

At the Headquarters, guards watch the main gate and courtyard, as usual. This was a place I practically grew up in, every part of it as familiar to me as if it were home: the wrought-iron gate topped with its warrior angels, the three-story stone buildings covered with ivy now glistening in the rain, and the cobblestone courtyard where we trained for hours. But today, I don't know if it's wise to allow anyone to see me here. Will they even allow me in?

But when one of the guards sees me there, he nods. I realize I know him and that he doesn't seem awkward about my presence, so I enter through the gate and across the courtyard without a hitch. Everything feels normal. I walk briskly through the headquarters' main hall to the library without any questioning, either. I guess the Duke hasn't sounded the alarm.

Inside the library, I make sure the way is clear. Fortunately, most contenders and Keepers are at the arena right now, and I have the place to myself. I have spent hours studying at these oak tables, but it was only the other day I realized the shelves hold much more than just books. I push a concealed lever embedded in one of them, revealing the hidden entry and secret stairwell to the Remedy.

Before going down, I listen for any sounds. But, if I'm honest, I have nothing to lose at this point. The stairwell is silent. I light one of the torches from the top landing before making my way down. The stairs don't seem to go on for so long this time around. However, the door engraved with the reindeer still feels much more alive than any door should. I force myself to focus on the lock, and the door is as I remember, insufficiently difficult to open for what it's protecting. I open the lockbox to remove my tools to work on the mechanism. I enjoy the task because it's something I'm good at.

It doesn't take long for me to succeed, and I'm back within the room of tapestries. I set the lockbox down on the central table and begin working on the cabinet guarding the blue glass flasks. When I open the compartment up and see all the Remedy in front of me, I realize the extent to which this is a treasure trove of possibility. It baffles me that this little elixir actually protects the Keepers from the creatures. The textbooks describe it as extracted from flowers, but I never was that into botany or pharmacology. Granted, it didn't quite work for me, but I guess it's because I have more issues than most people.

I tuck the tools back into my cloak, and then I reach for one of the flasks. My hand is shaking a little. I guess because part of me realizes what I'm doing is wrong, but under the circumstances, I find it justifiable.

I bring a flask to my lips, and once again the buttery honey aroma envelops me, blanketing me with comforting goodness. Where my loss of Uncle Felix was paralyzing, it's like I've been released and set free. As waves of blissful calm wash over me, I can breathe again and am even thankful the Duke brought me here. He didn't have to show me where the Remedy was, but for some reason, he did. I can't help but smile to myself.

After taking another glance at the shelves, I decide to take more. Why not? It will be like an insurance system—and who knows how the Remedy might come in handy?

At least now I'll have something of value to my name. I stash the flasks deep into my cloak pocket, the one not holding my tools. It's awkward and bulky and a bit difficult to carry without a satchel, but it will be worth it.

Before I close the door behind myself, I listen for sounds in the stairwell. Everything is still quiet, and I climb back up the stairs. In the courtyard, one of the guards flags me down. My initial instinct is to run, except that he smiles.

"I'm looking forward to your fight this afternoon," he says.

I smile back and nod, wondering if I could in fact still participate in my fight. No one seems to have any issues with me at the Headquarters, so maybe my problems are isolated to the Duke and I and the notebook. But do I even want to fight? Should I continue on with everything else, as if it was the same? I realize, why not? As I make the decision to still fight, a rush of adrenaline pushes through me. I almost have a skip in my step as I return to the arena for the contests.

Though the square in front of the arena is drenched, the festivities continue. Each row of booths is embellished with fall garlands made from leaves, pine branches, and streams of red fabric. Even a string quartet is playing lively music on a candle-lit stage in a main tent. People are excited and enjoying the occasion, eating, laughing, and shopping. As the day unfolds, everything seems to be as it should be here, nothing dampening their desire to make the most of the day—not even the rain. And, per tradition, the festivities will continue well into the night.

When I hear the cheers emanating from the arena, it causes my adrenaline to rush through me again, like the wild River Trent is coursing through me with its torrential power. This is my opportunity to show the world what I'm made of! The possibilities seem limitless. They will know I am a true Keeper.

As I approach the contender gate, however, there is an unexpected twist in front of the entry. I glimpse a black cloak billowing in the wind. The last person in all the world I want to see is standing there, his broad shoulders and stance like a rock, warning me not to approach. The Duke is watching for me. Maybe he thinks I might bring him the notebook. I don't care to find out.

I can't help but walk away, disappointed, but thankful the Remedy is shielding me. I could handle practically anything right now.

As I retreat into the market and wander around, I wish I could buy some food and a satchel, but I only have a few coins to my name. As I ponder my predicament, I happen to notice Molly toward the end of one of the rows, standing in front of a cheese vendor. Her presence takes me by surprise. I didn't think she would be back here after her morning fight.

I maneuver through the people toward her. If I can somehow recuperate the notebook, then I might have a chance at getting my life back. I double my pace, pressing forward through the crowd. When she pauses to adjust her satchel, I realize this is my opportunity. Likely thanks to the Remedy, I feel a surge of blind raw strength. I wrap my arms around her waist, pulling her in tightly to me and behind a booth.

"What's wrong with you, attacking total strangers?" she shouts at me.

I cover her mouth before she draws attention and turn her to face me. That's when I realize it's not Molly—this girl is older and her face is different. In fact, there is hardly any resemblance to Molly at all, except for the long chestnut hair. How could I have made such a big mistake?

I realize strangers are noticing us, which is the last thing I want. I let go of the girl and hurry away as fast as I can, into the tangle of neighboring streets, ignoring the shouts that follow me.

Afterwards, as I walk the streets, I decide to continue searching for Molly. I have no idea where she lives or where she might be, but finding her and the notebook seems like my only plausible way forward. For many hours, I scour through the city streets. A dozen times I think I see Molly's long hair, but each time I check, it's not her.

When it is well into the night and my legs decide they no longer want to move, I find a side street—a dead-end—and some crates to rest behind. I collapse against the wall, drop my head between my hands, and tears force their way down my face. I can't remember the last time I cried. And when my body begins to shake, I realize the Remedy may be wearing off. Will the withdrawals start to come now? It's going to be a terrible night.

CHAPTER 11
Molly

All I care about is saving my brother. He is the only family I have and the one person I care about more than anyone in the world. To me, he's the one individual worth fighting for, and if that means finding the Mirror of Sparrows, so be it. I can't turn in the notebook because, if the Duke were ever able to figure out the clues, he would have the Mirror. Who know what he would do with it? According to Hugo, there is a very good chance the clues to finding the Mirror are with me here, in the journal, and I am no longer concerned about the Keepers and their version of what is right or wrong. I need a place that is dry and where no one can find me, so home is out of the question. And so is the Keeper Headquarters library, where I usually study.

Keeping my face low and my head covered, I disappear through back roads. With the festivities, everyone is pretty distracted. Still, I don't want to stand out. I take to the garden rooftops, meandering between chimney stacks, chicken coops, and trellises covered with vines of vegetables and berries until I find a protective shed. It looks like it's mostly used to store gardening supplies, but it will do. Though a rainstorm begins to blow rather hard up here, the tiny shelter is remarkably cozy.

Searching for clues, I study through the pages of my father's notebook. I read and reread everything. Some of the writings appear to be journal entries, others poetry. If there is some sort of code, I'm not seeing it. But the clues must be in here somewhere, since Hugo was willing to break into the Duke's mansion for it.

I trace my finger along the branches and leaf designs. My father was an artist. And though I hate to think of anything he made as beautiful, I can't help but appreciate his skill. All the drawings appear to be different sections of one tree that begins on the first page and whose branches continue all the way through the book. It's pretty wonderful.

The more I study the art, the more it occurs to me there might be something more to it. A familiar pattern? Maybe the words are not the significant part of the book. Maybe the drawings are.

I take a deep breath. I need to think.

After looking over the depictions one more time, I see that the various design interconnect. I decide to break the threads holding the book together. If I'm wrong, it will be a drag, but I can just assemble the pages back in order.

I dig my knife out of my satchel. When I press it through the threads, it slices the stitching. With gentleness and trying to keep everything in order, I pull apart the entirety of my father's journal. I hope I am right, because the process is labor intensive and my last hope.

I sort the types of illustrations by categories: branches, trunk, outer edges of the leaves, some birds. I enjoy puzzles, so putting the pieces together happens naturally. As I find the proper places for each of the tree branches, the shapes they create bring to mind a familiar web of streets. It looks like my father disguised a street map of Saint Michael within the branches of this tree. After identifying the most recognizable avenues, as well as the River Trent, I work out the major landmarks.

But where is the Mirror? How will the map lead me to it? Besides the branches and leaves, little birds and forest animals, such as squirrels, adorn the tree. Stars and clouds also dot the sky surrounding the tree. But do any of these mean anything?

I pull out some of my leftover food to nibble on and contort myself to examine the map from different angles. Snug, in the midst of all the branches, sits a tiny nest with some baby birds in it. As I examine the illustration closer, I realize the chicks are labeled Molly and Hugo, with the shapes of the letters designed to look like little feathers. I might be wrong, but the nest seems to sit at the Saint Michael's Cathedral. That may not be where the Mirror is, but the place is absolutely significant and worth investigating. I have to see if there is anything in the cathedral for me to discover, so I fold the map and arrange the journal back into my satchel.

I peer outside for the first time in many hours and realize the sun will be setting soon. By the amount of water everywhere and the slick rooftops, the rain must have poured the whole day. With care, I climb back down to the street, trying not to slip or become too drenched. It's a hopeless cause, though, because by the time I make it down, my clothes are wet, and I've nearly slipped several times.

I make my way to the center of Saint Michael, where the cathedral spires rise high into the sunset sky, its roof glistening with brilliant mosaics of green, gold, and red. Because the cathedral is a sacred place, this is one of the few rooftops not used for food production—but it certainly works as a source of beauty.

I step through the massive cathedral doors. The priests are holding their final mass of the day, and the smell of incense and burning candles permeates the air. Matching the roof's color scheme, murals and carvings of tangled branches and birds cover the cathedral columns, vaults, and pews. The leaves start out green at the entrance and gradually turn to shades of autumn gold and crimson as they reach the heart and the altar. I remember how much my father loved this place.

I have no idea what I'm looking for, but I walk toward the front of the church and kneel in one of the pews to pray and finish the mass with everyone else. I fold my hands together and ask for wisdom.

When I open my eyes, I notice the engraving behind the altar, framed within ornamental branches:

> *Are not two sparrows sold for a small coin?*
> *Yet not one of them falls to the ground without*
> *your Father knowing. Fear not. You are of more*
> *value than many sparrows.*

The last line on the plaque catches my eye in particular: Fear not, you are of more value than many sparrows.

Though it might be sacrilegious to approach the altar, I have to see if there is anything back there, for the sake of helping my brother. So I wait until everyone has left, lowering myself between the pews, hoping none of the priests will notice me.

I shiver as the temperature drops, but I need to wait. After a long while, I decide no one remains except for me, and I walk down the center aisle, toward the altar.

Despite the obscurity, I can tell the sparrows' plaque appears set into the rock base such that something could be behind it. I run my fingers along its edges, testing for some loose parts. It gives just enough to offer me the hope that I might be able to pry it off. Good thing I have my trusty knife. It's coming in handy today. I insert the blade where the metal meets the stone and the plaque budges. Carefully, I work to move it, and like a little door, it actually swings open. I can hardly believe it.

My hands feel within the crevice and discover the hollow holds a wooden box. Will it contain the Mirror of Sparrows? Is it wrong for me, Molly Fitzpatrick—daughter of the thief and murderer of the previous owner of this precious object—to have this? I'm having second thoughts about my plan. But if I don't find the Mirror, how will I ever help Hugo?

After I take another deep breath and whisper one more prayer, I open the wooden box. Inside, a soft dark velvet wrap envelops something. My hand trembles as I pull away the fabric, and under it, to my astonishment, is the most sacred object in all the cities: the Mirror of Sparrows.

Few people have ever had the privilege of holding it, and so many are after its capacity to show anyone, anywhere, present or past—yet here it is, in my hands. I could literally ask it to see anyone.

I can't help but stare, even in the darkness. I pause for a moment to close my eyes. I don't know whether to feel happy and accomplished, or guilty and ashamed. After pulling my thoughts together, I remember Hugo and look at the Mirror again.

To see it properly, I borrow one of the many candles that adorn the cathedral and light it in a hidden nook. When I do, the Mirror magnifies the flame. The Mirror of Sparrows is simple but beautiful—not very big, in the shape of a square. The gold frame is composed of a tangle of branches and sparrows with emerald eyes, its style reminding me of Sir Jasper's glasses.

I need to test out whether the Mirror will actually work, though, but what should I ask to see? I'm worried about Hugo, of course, but it occurs to me to ask the Mirror about my mother. I haven't seen her since I was twelve. I could find out about her. Is she even still alive?

"Can you show me my mother?" I ask the Mirror.

It's a strange sensation, talking to an object. I wonder if it really will respond the way people say it should.

At first, nothing happens. Then, the glass's surface ripples like when someone throws a small pebble into a pond. I can no longer see myself in it. Instead, there is a woman with long, dusty-gray hair, and she is fast asleep. My mind is dizzy. My fingers tighten around the Mirror's frame. I can't handle this right now. Maybe some part of me didn't really expect to see her. I need to calm myself.

"Why did my mother leave Hugo and me?" I can't help but ask.

My worried reflection ripples away again, and my mother's face replaces it—this time, she is younger, with deep, dark eyes and a joyful countenance. The Duke, quite more youthful in this version of himself, as well, is speaking with her.

"If you don't leave them, their lives will be cursed," he says. "They will be shunned at every turn. You and your husband's legacy will poison them and be a dark shadow they will never be free from. But, if you move away from them—if you leave them—then you will be gifting them freedom; a new start, and endless opportunity."

A frown replaces my mother's smile, and the lines along her forehead and between her eyebrows crease.

That's not true, I want to shout through the Mirror. *Please don't go away.* Without her in our lives, everything worsened. *Why are you listening to him? We need you.*

"Why did she believe him?" I ask the Mirror.

Images of the Duke meeting with my mother repeatedly appear before me. He was relentless, and she was isolated, with two children, and no one to turn to. I guess, with my father imprisoned, Sir Jasper must have been at Saint Selaphiel, and presumably, the other Keepers, as well as her family, shunned her.

"The Keepers will take care of them for you," the Duke told her. "They will be better off without you."

I clench my jaw in anger. The only time we saw her after that was at my father's death, from a distance.

The Duke could only have had one objective: this Mirror. He knew my father had taken and concealed it. Divide and conquer.

"Show me where my mother lives," I ask. The glass settles on a plum-colored door, red flowers painted on its frame, and a small gold sign reads *250 Crumb Street*.

"Where is this place?" I ask.

From a bird's eye view, the Mirror shows me the city of Saint Selaphiel.

This is too much information all at once. I'm overwhelmed by the fact that I could actually go and find my mother. But I cannot worry about her mother right now. *Prioritize, Molly.* Hugo is the one I need to be concerned with.

"Please show me my brother," I say to the Mirror.

The glass in front of me ripples again, and my brother's silhouette appears against a roughly hewn, stone wall. He must be in a cell.

"Where is he located?" I ask.

The Mirror shows me the Keeper Headquarters, and then the image plunges down passageways within the depths of the building. I have never known or heard about what's below the Headquarters, but according to what the Mirror is showing me, a whole prison is down there.

"How do I get inside?"

The next image in the Mirror is of some keys dangling on a man's chest. He is scribbling notes and drinking a glass of red wine.

Of course I need keys; that seems plainly obvious to me.

"Who is that?" I ask.

The Mirror shows me none other than the Duke. He is much too dangerous.

"Isn't there any other way for me to access Hugo's cell?" I ask the Mirror.

The image changes to someone sitting at the end of a dingy alley, and as the picture focuses in on the person, a wave of uneasy recognition pulses over me. It's Colin, drenched and fiddling with some tools in a dead-end street, under some crates. How could this be? And why is the Mirror showing him to me?

"This doesn't make any sense," I tell the Mirror.

Then, it focuses on what Colin has in his hands. Are those lock picking tools? Could Colin help me break into Hugo's cell? Only two people in Saint Michael can handle pretty much any lock—Colin and his uncle. Everyone knows that. How could I have forgotten?

"What happened to him?" I wonder aloud.

This Mirror's reflection shows me Hugo and Colin on the bridge. They fight, and Hugo topples over the rail and hangs off the edge. Then, it shows Hugo and Colin again. They strike a deal whereby Colin helps find the notebook and Hugo never speaks about the bridge to anyone, ever. The reflection changes once again. This time, Colin's uncle is dying. Colin is with him, and the Duke orders Colin to find the notebook. And then, Colin steals and drinks what I can only guess is the Remedy. As my eyes attune to the details of Colin searching for me, an idea forms in my mind. It occurs to me I could give Colin the notebook, and in exchange, he could help me with Hugo. He wouldn't have to know the book is relatively useless and that I already found the Mirror, because all he wants to do is give it to the Duke. Neither he nor the Duke would ever know any better. It would be a win-win situation.

Would he agree to help me find Hugo? I think it would be a fair deal, his freedom for Hugo's. Maybe I can even give him the Mirror after Hugo is safe. But he can't know about it until then.

I ask the Mirror for clues on how to make the negotiation successful, but just as the glass begins to ripple, thunder crashes above the cathedral, as though the whole sky were imploding in an earthquake of sound. I think I've outstayed my welcome in this sanctuary. Before I wrap the velvet cloth back around the Mirror, I check the image in front of me one last time. It looks like it could be broken glass. I'm really not sure. But I don't want to stay here any longer. I slip the wrapped Mirror into my satchel, next to my father's disassembled notebook. I return the empty wooden box to its nest and force the plaque back into place. To my great relief, it sits perfectly in the stone groove and could pass for mostly undisturbed. I put the candle away, too, and make sure everything lies just the way I found it. After picking up the mess, I say one more prayer—this time of thanks—and head out.

It's been raining all night, with clouds so heavy over Saint Michael it seems like the sky could never have stars again. What a terrible night to not be able to go back home and have no place to stay.

By the time I spot Colin at the end of his dirty alley, he is soggy, miserable, and something moves near him—is it a rat? My goal is to approach with caution, and to somehow make it look natural. I want him to believe he found me.

I sit down at the beginning of the alley, hood low, and taking advantage of some nearby litter, kick over a discarded glass bottle. Hopefully, he hears it as it rolls and clatters against the cobblestones.

He obviously does because his eyes lift toward me. Even from the other side of the alley, they spark with recognition. It's unclear what his expression is because of his hood, except intense nervousness courses through me. What was I thinking, coming here to find him?

He approaches fast, like a massive advancing flood.

"Give me the notebook," he commands.

"I will, if you help me free Hugo first." I try to sound strong.

He rolls his shoulders back, making him look quite a bit taller, and his expression hardens. His eyes—red, tired, angry—are piercing.

"I've made enough deals with your cursed family," he says. "Hand over the notebook now. I know you have it."

From his cloak, he pulls out a sharp metal tool—maybe something meant for lock picking—and directs its point right at me.

"I want to help you," I say. "And I can give you the notebook, but you also have to help me."

With dizzying speed, he backs me up against the alley wall.

"That's not how this is going to work," he says.

"If I give it to you and you don't help me, that actually wouldn't be to your advantage," I say, desperate for a way out.

By some miracle, he pauses.

"Why?" he demands. But before I can answer anything, he tries to grab the satchel from me. I manage to slip it away from his grasp. I'm not just protecting the notebook now, but I must keep the Mirror safe as well. Hugo's life depends on it.

When he tries for the satchel again, I duck and snatch up the glass bottle lying by my feet. I hit the top of the bottle against the wall, and it breaks off, leaving a jagged edge. He freezes and fear flickers over his features. I take advantage of his moment of distraction to bolt away and up the neighboring crates to a window in the wall. He pursues me, and he is fast—except I kick crate at him as I climb.

Even though it's still very early in the morning, our fighting has drawn some attention, and a few passersby have gathered; guards have seen us as well. This situation has gone from bad to worse way too fast. Maybe I shouldn't have listened to the Mirror.

At the top of the mound, I cover my hand and punch a hole through the pane of glass to unlatch the window. As I fly inside, Colin springs at my heels, but just misses.

I scramble up a flight of stairs and run down a corridor. At the end, there is a ladder. I'm almost up, but Colin grabs hold of my ankle. The abruptness startles me, and before I can escape what's happening, I tip off balance and crash down, landing hard on my arm.

In the next instant, Colin has me in his grip.

"Give me the notebook," he says. "And I'll let you go."

As the sound of guards' shouting comes up the stairs in our direction, the pressure of choosing the right phrasing is on. I have but a few moments to convince him.

"Do you know why this notebook is so important to the Duke?" I ask him. That catches his attention. "It contains clues to the Mirror," I continue, "but the notebook will be useless to you without me showing you how to interpret it." And that's the truth. "You need me to understand it, and if you help me with Hugo, I will tell you everything. And if the guards happen to be after you the same way they are after me, then we are better off escaping them together instead of holding each other back." His eyes hold more curiosity than anger now. "The interpretation of this notebook," I continue, "is the key to your freedom and the key to finding your father's Mirror."

Colin's eyebrows furrow, and he pulls me up. "You'd better not be lying."

"I'm not," I say. "Please trust me."

He nods, jaw tight, but a flicker of trust passes through his eyes. After another moment's pause, we climb up to the roof together.

Guards below surround the building, and more are on their way up. I can tell because the sound of their shouts travels up from where we just exited. We are trapped among the rooftop vegetable gardens with seemingly nowhere to flee. To make matters worse, the storm clouds over the city rip open again, unleashing more wild flooding all around us.

"The river can take us out of the city," Colin says. "The gates are up because of the overflow, and the water can take us away from the guards and into the farmlands. And once we are there, we can hide, and you can tell me all about the notebook."

Has he forgotten his side of the deal? "What about Hugo?" I ask.

He clenches his jaw, but he nods as the guards' shouts sound closer. "We'll work something out."

He'd better help me, or it'll be his loss.

"The river?" he asks. "It's either that or the guards."

The image of Hugo in the cell flashes in my mind. What choice do I have? The river is close enough, so maybe we can make it if the gates are up.

When I nod, we bolt forward through the rooftop growth and downpour. The rain clings to my skin and soaks through my clothes, and we are about to be overwhelmed by guards. Somehow, we spring down to a back street, over slippery rails and running through massive puddles. We're barely outrunning the guards, but somehow, we've gained some ground, and I can hear the river. It's much louder than usual.

When we finally see it, the reality of our decision hits me like a punch in the gut. The river has massively swelled. The runoff and debris from the mountains crashes through the city and rages toward the bottom of the wall. I'm not sure if Colin and I can survive that. The water is as rough as it possibly can be, tearing against the banks.

"I'm not so sure I can do this," I say.

"This is our only chance," Colin says. "Think of Hugo."

Now he says that. I shake my head.

The guards advance toward us. By their shouts, louder and louder, they might be less than a block away.

I'm startled when Colin runs his fingers through my hair and unravels the long blue ribbon I had holding it up.

"What are you doing?" I ask.

"Tie this end to yourself," he says. With great speed, he attaches the other end to his leg. "We have a better chance of making it if we stay together."

Behind us, the guards call out. I glance back. They are rushing toward us, the satisfaction of victory etched on their faces. Time is up.

Colin takes one of my hands, while I cling to my satchel with the other, and we jump.

Maybe it would be fine if the Mirror and I ended up lost in the river forever?

The freezing water engulfs me into its heart-stopping clutches. Everything is chaos, except Colin is still clutching my hand.

CHAPTER 12
Colin

The water explodes with foam and chaos, and its currents yank me down. I try to relax my body and allow it to move freely, while still conserving air and gripping Molly's hand. Our only hope is to make it under the wall before the guards lower the gate, something knocks us out, or we run out of air.

The river shoves and twists me, then almost slams me against a wall—likely the city's fortifications. Molly's fingers slip from mine, but her ribbon still yanks at my leg. How long can it hold us together? I'm running out of breath and can't stay under much longer. I kick up to the surface and finally manage to push my face out of the water, sucking in a full gulp of air, just enough to refill my lungs.

The river drops, we veer to the right, completely changing course. Maybe we're going under the wall? The strong current pulls me through, ejecting me out of a tunnel. We must be safe from the guards by now, and the water settles a little. I surface again and take a deep breath. All around us are the farmlands.

I pull myself along the ribbon to reach Molly. She has made it, too. By her motions, she seems to be searching for something to hold on to. I swim to her, and after I find her hand, she finally notices me.

"We're through," I say. "Let's swim to shore."

The river, however, continues to push us forward and thickens again as the waters rush deeper into the farmlands. Brown water, branches, rocks, and debris from the heavy rains surround us, and a massive log courses toward me. It's getting close, and I ready myself and reach for it, but it's moving fast. When it's nearly in my grasp, the trunk shifts and swivels straight into me, knocking me in the side of the head. The shock is disorienting, and my vision blurs. Powerless against the water currents, my body is sinking, the world slipping away as I gasp for air. Then everything goes dark.

Water roars around me, and I can't tell if it's a dream or real. A desperate voice calls for me. Someone is shouting at me.

"Colin! Breathe," the voice says. "Can you hear me?"

A hand is holding me and pulling me up. My arms and chest are flung over a tree trunk, and we are racing down wild currents. Blood, a lot of it, is running into my eyes and mouth. It's all coming back to me: Molly and I made it out of the city, and then the log hit me. But as I find my bearings, it's not farmlands I see. Instead, walls of boulders surround us on either side, like impenetrable fortifications.

"Where are we?" I ask.

"Beyond the second wall," Molly says, a panicked look in her eyes. "When the log hit you, it knocked you out. Thanks to the ribbon, I pulled you in, and this log kept us afloat. I couldn't navigate us to the banks, though, because the currents were too strong, and then guards started chasing us again. I couldn't let go of you—otherwise, you would have drowned—and before I knew it, we were at the second wall. I've been trying to wake you up. I didn't know what to do. I had to take us under the second wall, but now, it's just a matter of time before the creatures find us."

"We're in the wilderness?" I ask, trying to process what is happening. "We went too far?"

"Yes," she says.

My freezing, numb muscles don't cooperate with me, and every jerk of the water puts me on the verge of slipping from the trunk—except Molly's still holding on to me. She props me up as best as she can, gripping me with one arm and keeping herself up with the other.

"We can't survive out here," I say.

But then, I remember all the Remedy I put in the deep pockets of my cloak. I wonder if it's still there. Molly and I are going to need it more than ever. I hold on to log with one hand, while I use the other to feel my pocket. Many vials are still in there.

"I know what we can do," I say.

Molly looks at me curiously. "What?"

"I have Remedy," I tell her.

Her features change from anxious to something else— I'm not sure what—but at this point, we can't afford to discuss the issue.

"Maybe we can try for over there?" I motion up ahead, to where water and branches are caught in a nook within the rocks, like a little cove.

Together, we kick in that direction. We don't have much time left before we drift past this outlet, yet we are hardly making progress. The log helps us stay afloat, but prevents us from going where we need to.

"We have to let go of the log," I tell her.

"You were unconscious just a few minutes ago. You probably have a really bad concussion. How can you make it?" she asks.

"I have no choice."

She nods and we push the log away. Instantly, the current pulls us apart, and the ribbon tying us together is taut again. As we swim to the edge of the water, menacing eyes stare at us—hungry, stalking, and powerful. While I don't perceive a body connected with the eyes, the rocks below them move, like something is clawing over them.

"Do you see that?" Molly asks. "We don't have fire."

"It's going to be alright," I say.

I tread water and pull three flasks from my cloak. I unseal the tops of two with my teeth, and throw their liquid down my throat. I hope that this time, it will work. I don't want to think about the after effects, not when, almost instantly, I feel calm and clear headed.

I hoist myself on to the riverbank and focus my attention on helping Molly. She needs Remedy, too, but she's still fighting her way over. Her face is taut with fear, her eyes searching the forest behind me. When she reaches for me, I find a solid foothold in the rocks and grab her hand. Though it's slippery, I manage to hold on to her fingers and pull her in close.

As she steps out of the water, I catch her in my arms, and her head presses into my chest. Her warmth reminds me of the last time Uncle Felix held me—like a little bit of home even in the wilderness. I can't help but draw her closer, clinging to her comfort. Maybe it's just the Remedy, but so what?

"Are you alright?" she asks.

"Yeah," I answer, though a nearby rustling brings me back to our reality.

"Here," I say, placing a vial into her hands. "It will protect you."

As I continue to hold on to her, the rustling grows louder, but before she has the chance to take the vial, a majestic reindeer with thick antlers that wind up high toward the trees steps out from the forest. It walks up over the rocks in front of us, and behind it, several more of the magnificent animals approach us. I can't help but stare. It's as if they are ushering us out of the river.

I glance at Molly. She's shaking with cold, but she doesn't seem scared anymore. She looks at the Remedy, then at the reindeer, and then returns the vial to me.

"I don't want to take it," she says. "I know what it does to people, and I'm not ready for it. Besides, the creatures haven't attacked me yet. Maybe it's enough that you have it. You can be my Keeper." She smiles. "I'm pretty sure the creatures would have destroyed me by now otherwise."

Am I keeping her safe? Is this how being a Keeper works?

CHAPTER 13
Molly

As my hands tangle into the back of his shirt, I suddenly realize how hard I'm holding on to Colin. He presses his face into my hair, and his arms tighten around me again. As I look up at him, however, his face is covered with blood because of a massive gash across the top of his head, and his pupils are wide. I'm startled because they remind me of my father's eyes when he would come back from his Keeper journeys between the cities. Inevitably, he would close himself in a room for a day or two afterwards, and we were not allowed to see him.

Despite Colin's warmth, it occurs to me that the true reason for his kindness is because he wants the notebook and the Mirror. I was so quick to almost forget about all the years he refused to have anything to do with me. With terrible reluctance, I ease myself out of his arms and back into the freezing air. Without him holding me, the whistling wind turns my wet clothes into an icy attack against my skin, and though I re-wrap my wet cloak more tightly around myself, my shoulders can't help but shiver and my legs burn with cold. I wish I could still be close to him.

"What's wrong?" he asks.

How can I tell him? All I want is to stay cocooned in the coziness of his arms, but I can't. I don't want to end up setting myself up for rejection again—especially not from him.

"Maybe we should step into the sun." He takes my hand and leads me into a patch of sunlight. In the rays, my body warms. The majestic trees frame the world around us, and below, a carpet of soft, green moss cushions our steps. The reindeer are still there, and Colin is smiling like I have never seen him smile before. I take it all in.

As I look at Colin's wound, though, the precariousness of our circumstances returns to me.

"You have a huge cut on your head," I say.

Colin feels the top of his head, and his fingers trace the edges of his wound.

"Let me help you," I tell him. I wish I could offer him stitches, but I don't have any supplies.

After he slices off a part of his shirt, I help him stretch the cloth around his head, securing it to contain the bleeding. His face is still bloody, so I take a corner of my cloak, and wipe as much of it off as I can.

"Thank you," he says, and my heart squeezes. I wish I knew what to say to him, but my tongue is tied. Instead, I see that the ribbon still connects us together. He notices, too, and lets out a little laugh.

"I can't believe it actually worked," he says.

"Me neither," I answer. "I'm grateful it lasted, though."

I kneel and begin to untie our exhausted connector. I realize that, with all my heart, I wish I didn't have to. It was amazing to be connected to him and to have the feeling that somebody didn't want anything to separate us.

As he unties his side of the ribbon, he looks up at me and our eyes connect, just like they did during the essay writing. But what had Sir Jasper told me? *Keep your wits about you. Focus.*

I go back to untying my side. After he hands me his portion of the velvet length, I wind it up and unfasten my satchel. As I tuck the ribbon away, I can't help but wonder what it will be like from now on between Colin and I, and my fingers start to tangle in the sash in my satchel. I almost lose track of my thoughts again, but I feel the other contents of my leather bag. That's when I remember the notebook and the Mirror. How could I have forgotten? Is the Mirror even still there?

I shift away from Colin and adjust my bag away from him. Incredibly, both it and the notebook are there.

"So, the notebook is still there," Colin says, his voice with a sudden intensity to it that takes me off guard. I guess I'm not as discrete as I think I am. "Does it really tell about the Mirror?" he continues. "I read through almost the whole thing, and I didn't see anything in it."

"Neither did my brother," I say.

His eyebrows scrunch. "But you figured it out?"

I can't help but smile.

He steps forward. "Molly, if you know how to find the Mirror, then we need to find it first. After that, finding Hugo will be easy. You have your priorities mixed up."

My stomach turns. The Mirror belonged to his father, so it *does* technically belong to him now, too, but if I return it to him, why would he ever help me find Hugo?

"No," I say. "First my brother, then I promise to help you find the Mirror. Besides, what would you use the Mirror for? Are you sure you just wouldn't turn it in to the Duke?"

His face pinches.

"After all, you have dedicated the last five years of your life to that man," I add.

He bows his head, and with a quick kick, flings a rock away.

I take a long look at him. The truth is, I don't see him the way Hugo does, but more like a young person, like me, struggling for his life.

"I guess we'd better make it back to the city then," he says. "But now tell me: you and your brother had this notebook all along?"

Colin has every right to react the way he does, and by hiding the Mirror from him, I'm more complicit than ever in the hurtful secrecy against him and his family.

"I didn't know about it," I say. I hate throwing the blame on my brother, but with regards to the notebook, it's the truth.

A darkened expression sweeps over his face, and he wraps his arms across his chest, hands under his arms, and looks at me with an eerie stillness.

"I just hope we find that Mirror before the Duke finds us," he says, then starts walking.

He begins to climb over the rocks, and despite his head injury, he moves with precision and agility. I need to keep up, but as I walk, my clothing and satchel are heavy with water, my cloak snags on seemingly every passing branch, and my shoes drag under me like a ball and chain. What weighs on me most, though, is a deep feeling of loneliness.

As the sun disappears behind the trees and boulders, I realize we're not making it back into the walls anytime soon. The river is almost impossible to follow because of the steep rock formations and the treacherous uphill trajectory. The frigid night is descending fast. With the plummeting temperatures, my body is stiffening, and my movements pain me. I am numb with cold, and the sharp rocks and tree branches create a difficult obstacle course.

As the darkness sets in, we come to a set of stone protrusions with what appears to be a little canyon running through it.

"Looks like we're not going to make it back tonight," Colin says, slowing down. "We need to at least try to warm up, and this place has shelter potential."

"I guess we need to build a fire," I say, irritated that every delay means increased risk for Hugo.

As we gather firewood, a light humming noise, like a groaning in the trees and in the rocks behind and ahead of us, travels through the gorge. There is no doubt he can hear it, too, because the sound echoes all around us. Even the rocks and branches seem to be vibrating from the noise.

"Do you think it could be creatures?" I ask Colin.

"I don't think they make that kind of noise, but just in case, I wish we already had the fire ready."

Colin and I proceed to pick up hefty tree branches off the ground and stand back-to-back, searching the darkness around us for movement as the humming approaches, ready to defend ourselves.

A person emerges from the rocks. His face is covered with hair, wildly overgrown and matted, and his hands are thick with dirt, with long fingernails clawing at the air in front of us. As he is coming toward me, I catch his eyes. The whites are a desperate and sickly yellow, and as he focuses in on me, he screams like it comes from the very depths of him. I've never heard anything quite so eerie before. In a frightening way, the sound resonates with the core of me. I wonder, could that be me one day? If the city rejects me, and if the creatures get me, this will be me. I could be just a few breaths away from becoming like that crazed person in front of me.

Side by side, Colin and I face the man, except several more people emerge from behind the boulders. Like wild animals, they crawl from behind the rock formations and surround us. We thrust our sticks toward them to try to keep them away, but I don't think this will do much good. I wonder what they want.

One of them lunges at us. Colin jams his stick into the man's face, and the attacker backs away. Meanwhile, three others encircle us. One of them tries to grab me—he reeks of rotten fish—but I knock him away with my elbow. When another comes, I take out my knife and thrust it toward him. At the sight of the blade, he backs off. To a certain extent, Colin and I are managing to intimidate them and keep them at bay, and we might be able to try to back away, except the steady rhythm of horse hooves suddenly carries over everything.

On horseback, appearing through the trees at the far end of the gully, another attacker charges toward us, thrusting a pointed wooden spear our way. Colin pulls a knife from the side of his boot and throws it at him, whipping it through the air. After the blade catches the rider under the collar bone, Colin bolts forward and seizes a tree branch. He rushes toward the struggling man, and plunges the wood into his gut, knocking him off the horse.

I grab hold of the mount before it escapes and, after swinging myself up on it, I turn the horse around and ride to Colin. One of the other attackers comes after me. Pouncing and holding on to my leg, he almost yanks me off. Meanwhile, Colin throws a rock at my attacker's head. I can't help but wince as the man falls to the ground.

Colin runs for me and the horse, and we manage to gallop off. Though our attackers' haunting shrieks pursue us, our new horse pushes forward and away, almost like he is desperate to leave as well. The cries fade behind us, but they are still frightening.

I take a deep breath and pat the horse. "Well done," I tell it.

My heart is racing, my hands are shaking, and adrenaline is pulsing through me.

After we have ridden what seems like far enough, I slow down so we can gather ourselves. I can hardly believe Colin and I are still alive.

"You saved us," Colin says, brushing his hand against the horse.

I'm not sure if he's talking to me or the horse.

"Thank God we had him," I say.

"And for you," Colin answers. He drops his forehead against my back.

I shift awkwardly and pretend to check on the horse. "Who were those people?" I ask.

"Aren't they those whose souls have been consumed by the creatures, but are still somehow alive? I have a feeling we may have come too close to their home—whatever that might be."

The image of the attackers and their wild eyes replays in my head, and the sound of their cries resonates in my mind. They embody the hopelessness I sometimes feel.

"Do you think they could ever become healthy again?"

"I don't know," Colin says. "I would hope so."

I'm surprised by his answer and want to ask him more, but he changes the subject. "I really wish we had something to eat. Maybe one of those loaves you always bake."

I shift awkwardly. Those were supposed to be secret.

"My uncle liked your bread," he continues.

"Did you?"

"It grew on me, eventually," he says.

"Really?" I can't tell if he's telling the truth.

"Honestly," he says, "the first time I actually ate it was the last loaf you brought us. But it was really good, and I wish I had tried it earlier. But I don't understand why you made deliveries like that. Who do you think you are, Saint Nicolas?"

I laugh. "I wanted to do good, especially to your family, but figured if you knew it was from me, you would reject it."

"I guess you were partially right, but maybe you worry too much about what other people think. My uncle loved your bread and never held anything against you. And think about your brother: he doesn't go around lurking in the shadows, and some people hate him, but many people like him. I know because it irked me."

I laugh. "I'll think about it," I say. He sounds just like my brother.

CHAPTER 14
Colin

Blood has saturated the fabric wrapped around my wound, and it's trickling down my face. Molly is barely managing to keep me on the horse as we weave between trees, directionless. Still, I keep pushing us deeper into the night forest, fleeing everything that's pursuing us. No matter how far we go, it doesn't seem far enough. Worst of all are the aches from losing Uncle Felix. The hurt pounds in my thoughts like the hooves of this horse beat on the forest floor.

My eyes close, and I almost fall off.

Molly catches me, wrapping her arms around me, holding me up.

"We have to stop," she says. "We can't keep going like this."

I slow our horse, and we ease down into the crackling of branches and leaves on the ground.

"I need a quick moment. Do you mind turning away?" she says.

"Why?" I ask.

"Bathroom break. I'll be just on the other side of this tree. But please, can you look the other way?"

When she steps off into the forest, the night sounds engulf me—the scurrying of small animals, a whoosh of wings, an owl's lone call. I am freezing without her, and shivers penetrate deep to my bones. A cold wind encircles me, whispering stories of deepest sadness.

From within the nearby trees, eyes stare at me—yellow and unmistakably hungry. They come nearer, and so is the sound of creaking, cracking branches. With trembling hands, I pull out a fresh vial of the Remedy from my cloak. I know it's not healthy to take so much, but what choice do I have?

I almost drop the vial as I uncork it, but after I gulp down the liquid, my heart steadies. At first, the eyes still linger, but then they begin to fade into the forest.

"Colin? What's going on?" Molly asks as she returns from within the trees.

"A creature was just here," I say. "Didn't you see it?"

She looks around. "No," she says. "Is it still around?"

Why did it approach me and not her?

"I took more Remedy, and it went away," I say. "We should be safe a while longer. At least the creature stayed away from you."

"That's a lot of Remedy," she mumbles.

I don't even want to think about what the quantity of Remedy I have in me now.

"What else was I supposed to do?" I say.

She shakes her head, then helps me climb back on the horse.

"Lean on me," she says, "and hold on." She pulls herself in front of me, and after that, she takes off, her direction purposeful.

After a little while, from under my bandage and hood, faint lights glimmer up ahead, illuminating what shimmers like water. We've hit a clearing. Unhindered by branches and trees, we travel through the field, fast. Tall grass sways around us, creating a dream-like world, and within it, a whole herd of reindeer gallops around us. The sky is saturated with an endless expanse of stars.

Up ahead, the reindeer are entering what I can only guess is a river. On the other side, I think I might see fires burning. If this is true, it may be one of the best sights I've ever seen.

As we approach the expanse's edge, however, the horse begins to slow down, and when we arrive at the water, he completely stops.

"I don't think he wants to go in," Molly says. "And neither do I, if I'm being honest. It's freezing, plus that water looks deep, and it's not a short distance."

We have to cross. This is our chance at survival.

I slide off the horse and approach our horse's face. "I know you don't know me," I tell him, "and that it's been a very rough day. I know I pushed you hard, but please trust me a little bit more."

The horse's ears shift forward as I stroke his face. He reminds me of Lightning, and I rest my head against his strong neck.

"We can do this," I say. "You are tough enough for this. I'll guide us through."

"But Colin, you're in terrible condition."

"I'm fine," I tell her and smile. "I feel good about this." Without the Remedy, I doubt I would ever be able to cope, but right now, it's empowering me—and so are the promises of fire and warmth.

As we follow the herd into the river, I lead the horse into the water, mud squishing under my boots and the horse's hooves. As I wade in deeper, past my waist, the icy water freezes my body. All my muscles want to rebel against me.

About half-way across, I have to swim. Everything except my head is submerged. The horse swims next to me. Molly's wrapped her arms around his neck and leans toward me.

"You alright?" she asks.

"We're almost there." I focus on the fires.

The horse swims more eagerly as we approach the other bank. I hang on to his mane, and soon enough, we are back on shore. My teeth chatter, but I know warmth is ahead.

The reindeer continue forward, leading the way to a cluster of homes—a tiny town. I don't understand how people have shelter and warmth here, or are even alive. It confounds me that we're in the middle of the wilderness, without walls protecting us, and yet here is what appears to be a functioning village.

The logs and rough stone houses have unusual moss-covered roofs, easily blending in with the surrounding woods. People come out of their homes and gather, watching us and the reindeer. Their eyes stay fixed on us, and some of them, I can't help but notice, are holding tools and items that could very well be used as weapons.

"Let's show them we mean no harm," Molly says, and then starts waving at them.

I'm not sure how reassuring that can possibly be, with us looking the way we do. The people, however, let us pass. They still don't approach us or talk to us.

"We need to ask them for some sort of shelter and help," I say.

"Let's try the place at the end of the way." Molly points ahead. "It looks like the main house."

Larger than the other structures, it's a two-story wood and stone home. Its roof is high enough that it blends in with some of the treetops. A few of the reindeer walk past us and nestle themselves among the trees nearby.

"Sure," I say. It seems as good a choice as any other.

After we make it to the front of the large house, we slide off our horse and tie it up to a rail within a nook of trees. As we do so, Molly approaches me, coming near to me, like she wants to say something but is hesitating.

"No matter what happens now or how everything turns out, I'm grateful for this time with you," she says as though this was the end of our journey—like she is saying goodbye. She reaches for my bandage and adjusts it, then uses her sleeve to clean some of the blood off.

"Are you planning on leaving?" I ask.

She doesn't answer.

Her lips are pale with cold. Her hair, loose from her braid and wet, clings to her face along with streaks of what must be my blood. The truth is that never, in a million years, would I have imagined she and I would be fleeing for our lives together. It has been the worst time in my life, but I'm thankful for her, too.

"We've survived a lot together." I take her hands in mine and pause for a moment, enjoying this closeness.

"We need to go inside," she says. "And we need to be able to explain ourselves. What should be our story?"

"Maybe we strayed from a caravan?" I suggest. It's the only idea that comes to mind.

"That sounds fine," she says. "I wonder what else could have happened to us?"

It's going to be interesting figuring out the details of our story. Molly and I are filthy and wretched, and our only hope is that whoever is in that house doesn't judge us too harshly.

Rough wooden steps lead to the carved front door. It has some sort of wreath hanging on it. I knock, and we wait. When Molly tightens her fingers through mine, I realize we are still holding on to each other.

An older woman with gray hair, bright eyes, a red dress, and an apron covered with flour opens up. At the sight of us, she takes a big step back.

CHAPTER 15
Molly

The woman that the Mirror has led me to is on the older side and has dark curly hair and a strong frame. She is someone people would think twice before messing with, though her long red dress and embroidered apron are unexpectedly cheerful and welcoming. Her eyes drift over my face and land on my burn mark. She pauses, though not for too long. Next, she takes in Colin's bandaged and bloody head.

"We're lost and really cold," I say.

"I can see that." She is silent for a moment after that, perhaps unwilling to abandon us to the wild, yet unsure about subjecting herself to our circumstances. "How did you get here?"

"Through the river," Colin answers.

The woman steps forward. "How did you survive this far into the forest?"

"We were traveling between the cities with the provisions for the Keeper contests," I say.

"Which city are you from?" she asks.

"Saint Michael," Colin says. "We had wild people and creatures come after us. We were lucky and found our way here."

"Lucky?" She laughs. "Luck could not protect you from the creatures or the Forsaken or the cold. Maybe the reindeer or some other powerful mystery might. But people don't just happen to wander this far from the cities and live to tell the tale. And, not only have you survived," she continues, "but you also found us. Explain."

Colin glances at me with a quizzical expression. I need to think of something, but what?

"We found a horse," I say. "And, from a distance, we saw the village fires—since it was night, the lights were easy to see." My explanation came out smoother than I expected.

"That still doesn't add up. How did you make it out of the city apart from the Keepers? The creatures wait for people like you to stray."

Why is she so intent on knowing all this about us? Can't she just let us in and talk later?

"In truth, we fell into the river, and it took us much further than we expected because of the flooding," I say.

Her expression softens. "So you weren't traveling with the Keepers, but you fell into the river? What am I supposed to do with the two of you?"

"If you don't help us, we'll die," I tell her, my voice shaking. Colin squeezes my hand. At least we are in this together, and I am grateful for his presence right now.

"We're just trying to survive," he adds.

She lets out a deep sigh and motions for us to follow her inside.

Colin and I look at each other with excitement, and we hurry in behind her. Against my initial doubts, the Mirror indeed found us a safe place. It was a risk using it near Colin, but thankfully, he bought my story about a bathroom break. Now if only Hugo could be safe, too. I clutch my satchel a little more closely.

As we enter, the smell of baking bread envelops me like I'm a dollop of butter that has found the perfect home to melt into.

"We left our horse out there," Colin says.

"We'll care for it, but first I need to deal with you," she says.

Herbs, garlands of ornamental pinecones, and dried wood pieces hang across the ceilings. The wood beams are carved with forest scenes and reindeer. On the far end of the room, a substantial fire crackles with two little animals—I'm not sure what—doze in its warm glow. A massive table, stacked with books, a burning candle, and the remnants of a dinner, fill the other side of the room.

"Take a seat while I'll find you some dry clothes and food," the woman says. "But if you are going to stay here, you'll need to give me more information. I need to know what I am dragging my village into, so think about what you are going to say."

Colin and I sit down right in front of the fire, and we stick our hands as close to the flames as possible. The furry animals opened their eyes when we came near them, but are now drifting back to sleep.

"I can't believe we found this place," Colin says, pressing his warmed hands against his cheeks. "Did you see her face when she saw us? I didn't think she would let us in."

"It is amazing," I say. I hope he doesn't think it's too incredible, though.

"How is it this village is safe within the forest despite the creatures?" Colin continues. "Since they don't need massive walls or guards to protect them, I wonder if they are also using Remedy. They must be, but I just don't understand how."

His mind is obviously spinning with questions, while mine is falling into the grip of anxiety. Between the Mirror and Hugo, what should I do? I'm further from my brother than ever.

"Did you see her reaction when you mentioned about the river?" Colin is still going. "I don't think she should know about the Remedy."

I nod. "But what about the Duke?" I ask. "Shouldn't these people have the right to know?"

"The Duke won't find us out here," he says. "We're too far. There's no need to complicate things."

Before I can contest, the woman reappears, carrying bowls of warm soup and a big bundle of clothing.

"Quite an adventure you two had." She stares at us intently as we drink the soups. It's a rich broth with some sort of grains, meat, nuts, and herbs. My insides warm from her wonderful provision.

"My name is Charlotte," she says.

"I'm Molly."

"Molly Fitzpatrick?" she asks. "I had a feeling."

My heart drops. How does she know about me, *all the way out here?*

"She's not who everyone thinks she is," Colin says between gulps of soup.

I glance at him, surprised.

"Is that right?" Charlotte says.

"And I'm Colin," he adds, as more blood trickles down his forehead.

"The washroom is there," Charlotte says, pointing to a door under the staircase, and she hands him a bundle of clothes. "Why don't you go first since you're bleeding everywhere."

Colin drinks down the rest of his soup and goes to the washroom.

As I continue eating, Charlotte sits down in a chair nearer to me and hands me some dry clothes, too.

"You care a lot about each other," she says. "Which is surprising, considering who you both are. Why did you two really leave the city together? I can think of very few reasons."

I want to squirm away, but resist.

"How did you know who I was?" I ask.

"Just because we live in the forest doesn't mean we are ignorant of what goes on in the cities. We stay in close contact with both cities. I've heard all about the Fitzpatrick girl with her scared face. Not only do I know who you are, but I know your friend as well—Colin Kelly, son of Kieran Kelly, the man your father murdered. Colin is the spitting image of his father—a face none of us will likely ever forget for those of us from Saint Raphael. Who knows what sort of trouble the two of you could bring."

"We mean no harm," I say. I don't know what else to tell her. I'm sitting here, wet, tired, and still cold. I can't think straight. But did she just say she was from the lost city of Saint Raphael?

"Your intentions might not match your reality," she says.

Thankfully, Colin comes back into the room. His timing was perfect. Was he listening at the door?

"Can you help?" he asks me. He is wearing the fresh clothes, but still has his filthy, bloody bandage around his head.

"I have what you need to fix him up," Charlotte says. "You, take a seat," she tells Colin. "Molly will be right back to help you."

She smiles and motions me back to follow her. I guess she wants to finish her line of questioning in return for the supplies.

We enter a kitchen filled with a blazing oven and stove, on which there sits a massive pot of heating water, and from what I can smell, several loaves are baking there, too. Thick wood counters, covered with carved bowls, iron pans, and dozens of clay jars, line the walls. How does she have all this in the middle of nowhere?

"You might as well change while I gather everything," she says.

"Here?"

"If you don't mind, that way we can keep talking. Just leave your wet clothes in the corner. I'll take care of them after."

As I change, I realize I have to pull off my satchel. It's unnerving, but I'll hurry.

Meanwhile, Charlotte goes to the far end of the space and opens up a massive armoire I hadn't even noticed yet. From what I can see, she shuffles through many different supplies and herbs meticulously packaged in labeled tins.

"What is all that?" I can't help but ask, pulling off my wet layers and trading them for dry ones before returning my satchel to the safety of my shoulder.

"These are all the healing supplies for our village. You came to the right place."

"How do you have all this?" I ask.

"The forest has much to offer," she says. "Once you become familiar with it. Many healing remedies can be found out here, but we also travel to the cities to restock, as well."

I feel a surge of hope. "Could you help us return to Saint Michael?"

"To make it to Saint Michael, you will have to go by river to Saint Selaphiel first, then find a Keeper caravan back."

"Why do you stay here if you can go back to the cities?"

"We have our reasons," she says.

After I'm changed, I come close to her and marvel at her collection.

"He's likely having trouble with withdrawals, too?" she asks.

How does she know about the Remedy? What do I say?

She smiles like she understands my predicament and pulls out some dried leaves. "We'll make these into a tea."

With a carved wooden cup, she scoops out some water from the big pot, then stirs the leaves in with a little copper spoon and takes in a whiff.

"This will be good. Have him drink it and it should help him feel better," she continues, handing me all the other supplies. "So, there are only a few ways to stay protected from the creatures—the worst being the Remedy, which Colin reeks of. It's a terrible poison, extracted from flowers in the forests by my old home. It is extremely dangerous. Now that he is safe, he must stop taking it. No matter how much he wants to take more, do not let him. Otherwise, he could die." She pauses. "This tea should help alleviate some of the withdrawals. Until he is through them, he will be more susceptible to creature attacks, and his body, mind, and spirit will become weak."

"How are you surviving the creatures?" I ask her. "And how have I survived? I haven't taken any Remedy."

"Colin has been your Keeper. So too have the water and the reindeer protected you," she says.

"I should have offered to take Remedy for Colin, but I was scared to."

"Rightfully so."

"What about the water and reindeer?" I ask. "How do they help?"

"Water and fire are poison to the creatures. The reindeer, they are like Keepers, too. They care for people. Aren't they the ones that walked you to our village?"

I thought it was just the Mirror. It never occurred to me the reindeer were protecting us, but all along the way, they had surrounded us and perhaps guided us.

"How do they do it?"

She smiles. "They see things we cannot, and the creatures fear them. You should be grateful they found you."

"Are they how you survive?"

"Yes. Plus, the creatures can't cross over water. That's why they can't attack us on these islands."

"How did you end up here?" I ask.

"We are originally from Saint Raphael. The Keepers forced us out. Colin's father tried to stop it, but as the story goes, the Duke allowed the creatures to breach the walls. The Head Keeper did the best he could, under the circumstances, but the task was enormous." She shakes her head as though reliving it in her mind. "We had to leave everything. We tried to make it to another city for safety, but while some made it, most didn't. Others were guided by the reindeer."

I can hardly process what she's shared.

"I never knew that."

"Few people do. And this history is why I need you to promise never to reveal our presence here. I will need Colin to promise, as well."

"The secret of your village is safe with me," I say. "If we make it back to one of the cities alive, I promise I won't ever say anything about you being here."

Charlotte hands me the tea. "And now, I have to finish up with some tasks in here."

"Thank you for your help," I say and leave her to return to the main room.

Colin is lying by the fire, eyes shut, with the two little woodland creatures curled up next to him. When I nudge him, he opens his eyes.

"Let me check your wound," I say.

When he closes his eyes again, I take it as permission to start. To unwrap his blood-caked scraps, I moisten and loosen the fabric because it sticks to his skin and hair. As I do, I can't help but take in his face; the lines on his brow, the dark circles under his eyes. After gently prodding the fabric, the scraps finally peel off. The blood flow has slowed, but the gash is jagged and deep. That log really did a number on him.

"Do I need stitches?" he asks.

"A few," I say.

"You know how?" he asks.

"Yes," I say. "And I have supplies."

I show him the alcohol, needle, and thread, and I offer him the tea. "And this will help with the pain, as well as withdrawals from the Remedy."

He frowns, but takes a long sip.

CHAPTER 16
Colin

"You told her about the Remedy?"

"No. She said you reek of it," Molly says as she disinfects the needle and thread.

The withdrawals are already clouding my thoughts and causing me nausea. But is drinking this strange tea worth the risk? I don't know anything about this lady. And how did Molly find this place, anyway? Is the Remedy warping my mind or could Molly somehow have the Mirror? I need to find out. She has her satchel still tightly tucked under her arm.

"Why do you always cling to your bag so much?" I can't help but ask her.

"My father's journal is in here."

But is anything else in there?

"And not only does she know about the Remedy, she also knows all about who we are," Molly continues.

"How?"

"She remembers your father from the lost city of Saint Raphael. She says you're his spitting image." Her eyes linger on me. "She seems to know our whole past, just like everyone else."

"Saint Raphael?" I wish I had more wherewithal to process everything.

Molly nods and examines my face and injury.

"You don't mind stitching me?" I ask her, not able to deal with tackling a whole complicated subject.

"This is going to hurt a lot, you know?"

"That's fine. Let's get it over with."

"I asked the woman about how the village stays safe," she continues. As she cleans me off with the alcohol, it stings badly.

"Apparently," she continues as she works, "besides fire, of course, the creatures can't touch water and are scared of the reindeer. Imagine how that knowledge could change everyone's lives?" She places a twisted cloth into my mouth. "Now bite down on this."

I want to ask more, but my words come out like muffled nonsense. Instead, I find myself holding onto her folded legs. It's the only part of her I can readily access.

"Are you ready?" she asks.

After I nod, she takes a deep breath and brings her needle near me. With her other hand, Molly holds the skin around my wound in place. I focus on the concentration-crease forming between her brows.

It hurts when she pierces my skin, but she has steady hands. While every stitch burns, it's not as painful as I had feared. I do, however, feel more and more dizzy and disoriented. It's becoming difficult to focus my thoughts. I wonder if it's the tea or the beginning of withdrawals. I think it must be the tea, because the withdrawals didn't do this before.

One stitch and knot at a time, Molly sews me up. Before I know it, she ties the last threads and removes the cloth from my mouth.

"Seven stitches," she says, cleaning the area around my wound again.

When I sit up and am facing her again, the room is spinning.

"Thank you," I say. "How bad does it look?"

"It just makes you look tougher." She smiles, and despite my drowsiness and nausea, I can't help but think about her scar. Before I realize what I'm doing, I reach for her face.

"How did you get yours?"

Her eyes fall from mine. "On the night the Keepers came for my dad, an oil lamp exploded."

"It makes you look tough, too," I say, unable to find words better suited to the situation. I wish my thoughts weren't in such a jumble.

"Except people say it was a curse because of what my father did to your family." She holds up the cup. "Do you want to finish your tea?"

"It's making me dizzy," I say, but I drink it anyway. "And just because people say something doesn't make it true."

"Don't you think it's true?"

I shake my head. "Maybe I did, but not anymore."

She sighs then starts up again. "Colin, I have to help my brother. I'm constantly worried about him."

"We'll help him," I tell her. "Don't worry. We're in this together."

"But you have to stay here and recover from the Remedy or you could die." She stands, wipes down her hands and gathers everything up.

"Are you planning to leave?" The reality of what she was saying suddenly hits me.

She stops. "I'll be back. You just rest and recover."

"Molly, we have to stay together. You need my help. Remember?"

"I'll be here for you, but I have to help Hugo, too."

She walks back to the door, even as I call for her. But I can no longer hold myself up. Instead, I lie back down in front of the fire, my eyes drifting shut despite the throbbing. At least I'm warm now—in pain, but warm.

I'm not sure how much time has gone by. Molly is lifting me up, and that lady Charlotte, too. They guide me up some stairs, and next thing I know, I'm between some clean covers.

"Molly," I start to say, reaching for her.

She takes my hand.

"Don't go," I say. Why does she want to leave so soon? What changed her mind about being able to do it alone?

"I promise I'll come back," she says.

I don't want to fall asleep, but I can't help it.

The Duke is in the room with me. He smells of cloves and too much wine, yet his eyes are unflinching and clear. He throws my lock picking tools on the floor.

"I'm upset with you, Colin. First, there's the whole issue of you breaking into my office, and you then steal the vials of Remedy. I treated you like a son. I trusted you, and you betrayed me."

The Duke takes my face in his strong hands. His fingers immobilize me and hurt my wound. He runs a thumb over my stitches. An awful taste creeps into my mouth, like I'm about to throw up.

"Too bad," he says. "You had such a nice face."

Next thing I know, I lean over and vomit all over the Duke's polished boots. He pats me on the back and finds a cloth with which to help wipe down my mouth, and then his own shoes.

"This will all soon be over," he continues. "I really want you at my side, but we have to hand the girl over to be punished. I've decided to ask the Keepers for another chance for you, but only if you give me the notebook and turn her in. You may have been the thief, but if you cooperate, she will go down as the guilty one."

"She's innocent," I say. But is she? Though it seems impossible, she might have the Mirror—but she's not like the Duke, and she's not the one who killed Uncle Felix. "You can't do that to her."

"Things will be better that way."

I startle myself awake and open my eyes. I realize I have been asleep and dreaming, but the dream is still playing in my mind, and I am scared. Something is wrong. *Where is Molly?*

CHAPTER 17
Molly

Within moments, Colin is fast asleep. The room Charlotte directed us to has two beds with matching red and green patchwork quilts. He is shivering under his cover, but Charlotte is igniting a fire in the stone fireplace at the back of the room. The floors and walls are all made of rough wood, but it's really cozy. The place is simple and decorated with an assortment of forest treasures, similar to the room downstairs.

After our host leaves, I stretch myself out on the other bed. I need to sleep, but will leave well before dawn. All I can think about now is helping Hugo. After checking the Mirror again and seeing how sick and beat up he looked, I know I have to hurry.

I take a long glance at Colin and wonder about my plan. Is it bad for me to leave him while he is recovering?

And I'm conflicted about keeping the Mirror from him, too. But Hugo's life is at stake.

Hopefully, the reindeer will help me, but I don't know. Will I be able to make it back? And what about the Remedy? Colin needs to stop taking it, no matter what. Maybe I should take it with me, just in case?

I peer out the window, trying to gauge the time. Everything is still dark. Thankfully, I haven't overslept.

Once I'm ready, I check the pockets of Colin's cloak. A number of glass bottles clink together, and I pull one out to see. It's a full blue-glass, corked vial. I decide to take all of his stash, that way, he can't have anymore. It might not be the best decision, but right now, it seems like a decent idea. I try to load them into my satchel, but they don't fit.

I have an idea. I clear a place in my satchel by removing the notebook and tucking it into Colin's cloak pocket— where the Remedy vials were. It seems like a good trade.

After that, I add another two logs to the fire to make sure the room will stay warm until morning, and I also take the quilt off my bed and lie it over Colin. Once he's well tucked in, I tip-toe out and down the hallway to the top of the staircase. I slink down the stairs and am about to head toward the front door. Just then, I notice the kitchen door is open. Would Charlotte stop me if she saw me? I continue to creep out as quiet as I can.

Outside, cold air and darkness envelop me. It has started to snow. I wish I could have stayed inside, in the cozy bed. It will be a long journey to Saint Michael.

When I trek around the back of the house to see if I can find the horse Colin and I rode in on, I think I hear someone behind me, but when I turn, no one is there. I do see a stable, nestled within a grove of pines. Inside, our horse is there, among several others. He's not too happy about me waking him up this early and pulling him back into the cold. I bet he was really looking forward to sleeping in, too.

I pull out the Mirror.

"How do these people travel off this island?" I ask. "How do I make it back to Saint Michael?"

The Mirror shows me that, at the far edge, a barge connects the island to the bank of the river with a rope and pulley system. It also shows me some canoes. Considering I have the horse, the barge seems like the better option.

After following a well-worn forest road, I arrive at the water's side to find the promised transport. My heart skips a beat. With the help of the Mirror, maybe I truly can succeed.

The truth is, while I may be safe on this side of the river, the creatures will be hunting for me as soon as I cross. As I prepare to embark, I'm not sure whether to take the Remedy. If I do take it now, how much? I pull out a flask, but don't feel ready for it. I guess after seeing what it did to Colin, the withdrawals are not something I look forward to.

The horse and I approach the barge. He shakes his head at me, and I have to coax him on with much cajoling. I wish I had a treat for him, but I didn't even think to pack food for myself.

The platform is rather unsteady, but we manage. I hope I'm strong enough to make the pulley system work. As I pull on the rope, wet and slippery in my hands, the water moves gently under us. Soon the momentum helps us forward, onto the middle of a glassy expanse and into a dense fog. I squint my eyes in hopes of gathering clues as to how much further I have to go, but it doesn't help.

I'm in the thick of a dense cloud, and I cannot see across the water.

After I travel a little farther, the outline of the riverbank and forest begins to appear. *Should I stop and take the Remedy?* Yes. I must. There is no more putting it off. It's too risky to hope for reindeer. Except, just as I am about to take out one of the vials, I realize there are silhouettes up ahead that look like reindeer. Could it be? Maybe I will be fine?

The next thing I know, my barge is moving forward on its own toward the shore, without me pulling the rope. That's when I realize the silhouettes are not reindeer, but people on horseback. They are pulling me in. I try to stop the forward motion, but they are too strong. They drag me ahead, faster and faster. My heart is beating so hard I think it's going to explode.

"It was just a matter of time before we found you," someone calls out from behind the thinning haze. I don't need my eyes to recognize the frightening voice.

I move to the rear of the barge. My only hope is to jump into the freezing water. My body knows the truth of how cold and torturous it will be, and my muscles seize up. I don't have a choice, though. If the Duke catches me, it will be the end, and he will not only take me, but the Mirror this time, too.

I think of Colin leading me through this icy river just a few hours ago. Despite his wounds, he pressed forward, and the picture of him forging ahead gives me strength. Leaving the horse behind, I grab hold of my satchel and plunge into the water.

The river is just as cold as before, maybe even worse this time, but I swim back toward the shore as fast as I can. There, I crawl through the mud and pull myself across reeds and hoist myself over a fallen trunk. I consider hiding there but realize that won't work. Instead, I begin to run through endless clumps of tall grass and trees, toward the village.

It hits me then that I am leading the Duke and his guards to Charlotte and her people—exactly what I just promised not to do. And not only am I taking the Duke to the village, but also to Colin.

It's too late now. Several of the men are already on the island behind me. I can hear them.

Distracted, I stumble forward, flying head over heels and land hard on to the ground. I must have tripped over protruding roots or a rock.

Within moments, the Duke's guards encircle me and, next, the Duke himself walks his horse through the grass to tower above me. He puts the tip of his sword under my chin, pushing it up, just like he did before. Only this time, Sir Jasper isn't here to protect me. I feel like a scared child.

"Do you have the notebook?" he asks.

I really wish I hadn't left it with Colin and that I could just hand it to him right now.

"I don't have it," I say.

What if he finds the Mirror on me instead? It's almost inevitable. His one ambition in life is the Mirror. I can't let him discover it.

Somehow, it occurs to me that the guards probably wouldn't recognize it because the Mirror is not what they're looking for. So long as the Duke doesn't see the Mirror, then this predicament could be all right. But how?

I take my carry bag from my shoulder and thrust it toward one of the guards defiantly. "See for yourself."

He grabs the satchel and dumps out all my belongings: the Mirror, my clothes, the flasks of Remedy, the ribbon that had held me and Colin together, everything I have with me. It is now but one big mess of a pile on the forest floor.

The Duke glances down at it. Something catches his eye, and my heart squeezes with fear. He leans forward, and out of the pile, he picks up a flask of Remedy.

"Thief," he says. "Where did you find this?"

My shoulders relax. That was too close, but who would have thought the Remedy would have helped me in this way?

"Like father, like daughter. I'm not surprised," the Duke continues.

Several of the other men come nearer. Their features are worn, just like Colin's, with deep circles under their eyes and sunken cheeks. They must have used a lot of the Remedy to follow us, and it must be taking its toll on them as well.

Two of them sift through my small pile of possessions, but they have no idea they are in the presence of the Mirror of Sparrows. Meanwhile, the Duke is more preoccupied with the Remedy than my pile of stuff.

"She doesn't have the notebook," they say.

The Duke yanks me forward. "But you'll help us find it, won't you?" he says. "And where is Colin?"

The Duke knows I'm not alone, and it's only moments before they discover the entire village.

Thankfully, as they take me with them, they leave my belongings. The Mirror also remains on the forest floor, half buried in the layers of dead leaves and dirt. What if it stays lost here? At this point, losing the Mirror once and for all might not be the worst thing.

CHAPTER 18
Colin

Where am I? Sweat soaks my sheets, my head throbs, and my body aches. I cautiously sit up and take in my surroundings. Everything is a little blurry. The bed beside mine is empty. Several quilts cover me, and a fire is crackling in the hearth near me.

How long have I been asleep? Events from yesterday come back to me: the river, the forest, the attacks, the stitches, Molly. My head throbs as I pull myself out of bed and reach for my belongings. My clothes hang on the chair by the fire, and they are almost dry. I search around the insides of my cloak, wanting to take inventory of what I have.

Instead of my glass vials, I find a leathery notebook—the Fitzpatrick notebook. Why? Where is my supply of Remedy?

I stand abruptly and glance around the room. It hits me that the quilt that was on Molly's bed is now on my bed and that nothing of hers is here. I push my fingers through my hair and try to wrap my head around this. Did she really leave?

I head out of the room. As I approach the stairs, boisterous voices rise up from down below. A handful of men eat around the table in front of the fire. I know these people: the Duke's Keepers, the ones he trains at his mansion. And one person sits facing the fire. Though his back is to me, I would recognize him anywhere. It's like my heart stops and I freeze.

The Duke has found me.

I wish I had time to escape, but he turns to me, his face both demanding and unreadable.

"Perfect timing," he says as he pulls out his gold pocket watch, as though he has actually timed any of this.

"Come and sit with me." He motions me downstairs and points toward a chair near himself.

I want to run, but my feet refuse to budge.

On the stairs, the lady who helped us last night—Charlotte I think was her name—climbs past me. "Good morning," she says, a sarcastic tone saturating her words.

I try to calm myself, but my thinking only becomes more strained. When I reach the bottom of the stairs and walk up to the Duke, all I focus on is, *this man killed Uncle Felix*.

"You might be happy to know, we've found Ms. Fitzpatrick," the Duke says. "It seems she abandoned you out here, stealing all of your Remedy." He places the vials on the table for me to see, as if to show me proof. "I don't know why you thought you could let your guard down around her. Don't you remember who she is?"

Did Molly really take the Remedy and leave without me? I'm not sure what to think about her, except that she helped me survive yesterday. What I do know is the Duke is here not for me, but because he wants the notebook, and ultimately, the Mirror that once belonged to my father.

The Duke stands and leans in close to me. He smells like he did in my nightmare.

"For you to receive pardon, just turn in the notebook," he continues. "Since the girl doesn't have it, I'm guessing you do. So, let's settle matters now."

"What about Uncle Felix?" I challenge him. "How are we going to settle *that* matter?"

His expression sours. "Your actions had consequences, and your uncle's death was the direct result of your betrayal. Do you have the notebook?" the Duke repeats, more sternly this time.

I remain silent. There is no negotiating with him. I have nothing to say to him.

"You fool," he says. He shakes his head and motions to his Keepers. Two of them approach. "Whatever happens to you now, you have brought this upon yourself. Search him and his room."

One of the Duke's Keepers—Charles—grabs me by the upper arm, his grip unnecessarily tight. I trained with him, but now, his eyes hold nothing but contempt for me. When I shove him away, another Keeper grabs hold of me. Together, he and Charles pull me through the front door. Snow has started coming down, and the pine trees, ground, and rooftops glisten with a glaring white light. There are several other Keepers out here, too.

I'm still feeling weak from the journey here, and I just wish this all would end. Maybe this isn't real and I'm still asleep, but the cold dirt, leaves, and snow under my feet tells me otherwise. Now is not the time for me to falter. I need to be strong and smart.

"Where's the notebook, Kelly?" Charles walks up to me and jerks my face toward himself.

I toughen my stance and stare at him.

"Search him," another Keeper orders when I don't answer. Several of Duke's Keepers proceed to pull off my new woolen clothing, then shove me to the ground. I try to fight back, but I am outnumbered.

"Where is the notebook, pretty boy?" Charles is now holding a bucket of water. If he throws that on me, I will freeze. But I don't say anything.

They shove me to the ground and kick me. How can they call themselves Keepers? I have no protection and am completely at their mercy while they laugh, taunt, and kick.

"Where is the notebook, Kelly?"

"Traitor!"

"This is disappointing for the son of a former Head Keeper!"

When I don't say anything, they dump the icy water on me. Like it's a frozen sack of potatoes, they push my body around and drag it over the glacial ground. As they do, I force myself to examine their faces. I study each one of them, committing their features to memory. They are red, not with cold but with drunkenness of violence, more beast-like than human. My only comfort is to know that if I escape this situation, I will do everything in my power to hold them and the Duke accountable.

"We found the notebook," someone shouts from the house. "The Duke says to bring that worthless traitor back in."

Charles throws my now wet clothes back at me. My body aches and shivers as he pushes me back inside, up the stairs, and back to what was my room. I can barely think straight or stand upright. In the room, broken furniture, blankets, and shattered decorations and things lie across the floor. They've ruined Charlotte's home, and who knows what they will do in the village. Nothing is where it was when I had left it, and the notebook and my cloak are gone. Although that's probably what saved me.

"Enjoy your final moments of freedom. Don't try anything, though. Everywhere is guarded. If you run, you'll never make it. If the guards don't kill you, the cold and these forests will. The creatures are hungry for you," Charles says with a grin as he locks the door behind me. I can't believe he was someone I had respect for.

It is true that, without the Remedy, I am a lost cause. I wrap myself in the quilts that were on the bed, now on the floor, and see some matches to restart the fire in the little fireplace. Once it's going, I sit as close to the flames as possible. I really need dry clothes. Then I realize that on the floor, strewn here and there, are my clothes from yesterday. Thankfully, they are quite dry now, and I gratefully pull them on.

I sit on the floor in front of the fire and wrap my arms around my knees with the blankets around and on top of me. The growing glow of the burning wood fills the little room and begins to warm me. As I stare into the rising golden reds and oranges, tears drip down my cheeks. The fire and the quilts remind me of Uncle Felix. I wish I could talk with him. What would he tell me right now if he were here? Uncle Felix was a master craftsman and problem solver. There was no lock he could not open, and no situation he could not navigate.

My eyes sweep across the chaos of the room and the mess scattered across the floor. There must be something I can do.

I go to the door and, through the keyhole, peer out to the hallway. Charles still stands watch. Though it would be crazy to attempt to escape him and this house full of guards, I have nothing to lose.

I thought I saw something earlier but dismissed it: several thin sticks of metal. I'm not sure where they came from—if anything, it looks like someone put them here. Charlotte? Is that possible? I don't understand why she would try to help after all the trouble Molly and I brought down on her.

As I sit in front of the fire again, I toy with the metal, bend and straighten into a more usable shape. These could be my ticket to freedom.

As I work, I wonder what happened to Molly. We did survive the river and forest together, after all. And does she somehow have access to the Mirror? And if so, what if the Duke gets a hold of it?

"They're bringing the girl up," a guard shouts from downstairs.

I hurry to the keyhole and see Charles leave my door and heads for the stairs. This is my "Uncle Felix" moment. The tools aren't quite ready, but this may be my only opportunity.

I insert the metal rods into the lock, and I guess my uncle would not be disappointed because I'm rather fast at unlocking the door. Though, to be fair, the mechanics of the lock are as basic as it gets. Still, I know Uncle Felix. If he is looking down on me, he would be proud.

I close and lock the bedroom door and disappear into a room across the hall. The room is similar to the one I just left, except this one has a striking blue color scheme to it. Charlotte has a nice set-up for being all the way in the middle of the forest.

Pressing my ear against the door, I hear Charles and the other Keepers joke with each other in the stairwell as they come back up. Thankfully, when Charles returns to his post, he doesn't realize I'm no longer in the room.

Unfortunately, people approach the door to my new room. A key is in the lock, and I hurry to hide myself under the bed. Though the length of it covers the entirety of my body, I wonder if this hiding spot will be good enough. My heart thumps fast.

Two people enter. I can tell one is the Duke by his voice and his shoes. The other person is Molly. Even though she hasn't spoken, I recognize her worn boots and mud-trimmed cloak.

"You can leave," the Duke says, and the door slams.

A chair crashes to the ground.

"You're not going to get away with this," he says. "If you don't show me how to read your father's book, you and your brother will suffer the consequences."

At least I know that if Molly does happen to have the Mirror, the Duke doesn't know about it.

There is a loud thud on the bed. He just sent Molly crashing against it. Should I try to fight him? But then more guards would come.

"You can't bully me," Molly shouts at the Duke. I don't know if I would have the courage to address the Duke that way.

The Duke laughs. "Actually, I can," he says.

She lets out a yelp and stumbles backwards. What is going on? My stomach squeezes. I want to grab him by the legs right now and get him away from her, but I don't want to make our situation worse.

"He's gone!" Charles shouts from the hallway. He pounds on the door. "He's gone!"

"What do you mean?" the Duke bellows, hurling something at the door—probably the already broken chair.

"Colin is gone!" Charles shouts again.

"Wipe that smirk off your face," the Duke growls at Molly. "This place is surrounded. We'll find him. And after we do, we'll finish what we started here. I'll teach you both a lesson."

The Duke leaves the room. The door slams and there is a turn of the lock.

I slide out from under the bed.

Molly jumps back in surprise, her eyes wide with disbelief. She's unmistakably taken a beating of her own.

"What are you doing here?" she asks. "And what did they do to you?" She comes near me and looks me over, checking my face and pausing over my stitches.

While I'm happy to see her, I'm angry, too. "Where did you go this morning?" I ask her. "And did you take all the Remedy?" I can feel my voice increasing in volume and need to make sure we are not heard.

Molly focuses outside the window.

"I thought we were a team," I continue at a whisper.

"The only reason we are a team is because you want information about the Mirror," she says.

"Initially, but that was our deal. I trusted you."

"I told you I had to help Hugo."

I shake my head at her. "You can't help Hugo if you're dead."

"I'm sorry, but it was what I had to do." Her face is set.

"We lost the notebook," I say.

"Everything I had—including the Remedy—is in the forest, on the other side of the island. But we don't need the notebook," she says. "I know all of the information we need by heart."

I consider her for a long moment, surprised on several levels. How can she be so dismissive of her father's notebook? And how can she be so confident about its contents?

"Let's get out of here, then," I say and carefully peering out of the window. How else am I supposed to respond? "How many guards were down there?"

"There were at least three in front."

To my astonishment, no one is below our window or this side of the house. They must be on the other side, but that likely won't be the case for long.

"The steep pitch of the roof looks tricky," Molly says.

"We have to try. This is the only opportunity we're going to get." I open the window.

"I don't know if I can."

"I'll help you. Remember the river, that was much more dangerous."

"We're up pretty high."

I reach for her hand and climb out. She's a little shaky, but takes it and crawls out after me. I hold her next to me, and we slide down the snow dusted shingles. Somehow, we manage to jump to the ground, landing in the snow and leaves at the foot of the house.

"See, that wasn't too bad."

She shakes her head. I'm not sure if she's agreeing with me or not. At least we both made it out.

When the silhouette of a guard passes us, I think that he will see us. Anyone who looks at the roof will see something big came out of the window. Thankfully, his mind is elsewhere, following older tracks, perhaps made by other patrols, and he doesn't notice us or the roof. After he passes by, Molly takes my hand, and we slink between the wall and the snowy shrubbery, then dart to the stables.

Through the door, making sure we hear no guards inside, we proceed carefully. Hefty horses in each of the stalls munch away at their hay.

A side door opens. Someone has entered the stable. Molly and I scurry into an empty stall, ducking behind its half-door.

The neighboring horse keeps on looking at us, though, and I am worried it is going to give us away. There is nowhere left for us to run. Footsteps approach. A hand appears from behind our partition, pulling it open.

Charlotte's lips form a grim line. She motions to us to keep silent and settles the neighboring horse with a pat and a treat.

"I'm sure glad to see you two made it out," she says. "Now, let's get you off this island."

"Why are you helping us?" I ask.

"At first I wasn't sure about you, but I've decided I like the pair of you. I see hope when I look at you." She smiles at us. "Now make it to the water, to the river," she says as she points through the forest. "There, we have canoes."

"I need to find my supplies first," Molly says. Her face is lined with worry.

Charlotte places her hand on Molly's arm. "My grandson was able to collect your belongings from the forest," she says.

"He was?"

"Your satchel and its contents were in the dirt, but they survived."

Molly's face pales, but when Charlotte hands her satchel to her, Molly eagerly takes a inventory of her possessions. I try to look too, to see if I spot any Remedy. Unfortunately, I don't see any of the vials. How are we going to survive?

"Thank you." Molly has brightened more than I thought possible and embraces the woman with a big hug.

"Is that everything?" I ask. What's the big deal?

"And here are some food and fresh clothes for you as well," Charlotte says. "And remember, the creatures cannot cross water, so as long as you stay on the river and its little islands, you'll be fine."

"Now I think I understand why the Keepers have those archaic rules about all contenders needing to know how to swim," Molly says.

"This plan doesn't sound fine to me," I can't help but say.

"It will do. Trust me. That's how we've survived. Some years ago, Keepers stole everything from us—our homes and land," she explains. "We were originally from Saint Raphael, but we still made it—thanks to the reindeer and the river—and we're still here."

"I thought it was the creatures that destroyed everyone," I say.

"The creatures were enabled by certain greedy people. Your father, Colin, tried to stop it, but he paid dearly. You must continue what your father tried to do. Do not let the Duke win. I think it's he who controls all the land we used to have, and that is where he grows the plants to make the Remedy. Now, it's time to go.

"Walk straight through the forest, that way. When you reach the water's edge, you will see several canoes. Take one of them through the way of the islands. The river goes all the way to Saint Selaphiel. Follow it there and help restore the Keepers and the Seven Cities to what they once were."

CHAPTER 19
Molly

I'm tremendously grateful to be back with Colin. I wanted to hug him so badly when he popped out from under the bed, and by the warmth in his eyes, he was happy to see me, too, but by his words, he felt deeply betrayed I left him. He just doesn't understand about Hugo.

I can't believe we made it out of the house. Even though the odds of us escaping were slim, it seems that when Colin and I work together, anything is possible. And Charlotte—she knew I had the Mirror, yet she gave it back to me. I hardly understand. She told us so much, helped us so much, and gave us too much to think about. I hope we can succeed and help make her requests come true.

After Colin and I rush through the forest to the opposite edge of the island, we find three wooden canoes, just like Charlotte said. They are carved with intricate leafy designs winding outside and inside of the frame. Colin seems instantly mesmerized by them. He passes his hands over the engravings, examining the construction and details of the boats.

"We better hurry," I tell him. This will be my first time ever on a boat, unless you count the barge from yesterday, and I've never met anyone who travels by water or sea. Most people are scared or just don't have the chance. "How do you think we're supposed to do this?"

"We'll figure it out."

Together, we pick up one of the canoes—the one Colin seems most enamored with—and haul it into the water. We climb in, holding on so we don't flip the whole thing. As his hands and arms grip mine, I feel safe. His face, his presence, the whole of him, as wrecked as he looks, are a steadying presence.

Having stabilized the canoe, we sit opposite each other. The earthy smell of the carved wood envelops us and helps me relax. After I place my satchel at the bottom of the boat, between my feet, Colin hands me an oar and takes another for himself.

Quickly, we realize our paddling doesn't work so well, and we coordinate our strokes to match. At first, I enjoy watching the oars plunge into the river and the glimmer of water flowing fast under us, but soon, the novelty wears off. How long will we have to row for? We should have asked Charlotte for more information. Granted, we didn't have much time.

The temperature is dropping. It hasn't snowed again, but the ash sky seems wanting to unload. It feels as though Colin and I navigate endlessly through a maze of tiny islands, each of which is thickly covered with trees and brush. It's beautiful, and I had always wanted to see what the wilderness looked like, though this is far more than I would have ever bargained for. I haven't seen any reindeer, either. I had hoped some would travel with us.

As Colin and I push our oars through the water, the relentless paddling and fleeing is exhausting. My body is deeply hurting, and I am seriously depleted, having not fully slept well in two days. I wonder when we will be able to rest. At least Colin seems to have a good sense of direction, but I wish I could check the Mirror.

"Do you think we lost the guards?" I ask.

"I doubt it. It's just a matter of time before they figure out what happened, and they'll be traveling on horseback," Colin's tone sounds short. He doesn't seem to want to talk. On top of that, his mannerisms are more and more shifty and unsettled—very much like how he was back in that rat infested alleyway. And even though it's cold out, he's sweating profusely. I am beginning to wonder if the withdrawals from the Remedy are returning. I wish I could have asked Charlotte for more of that tea for him.

"You stole from me," Colin says out of nowhere, and his muscles flinch with anger. "You took all the Remedy."

The tone of his words startles me, and my stomach clenches. "Charlotte said if you continue to take it, it will kill you."

"Don't blame Charlotte, and don't pretend like you were protecting me. You just wanted it for yourself so you could help Hugo." He pauses his rowing and stares at me, his face sharp, and his eyes fiery. "And, by the way, even if part of you did happen to be thinking about me, what I choose to do is none of your business."

I hate everything he just said, but if I'm being honest, he's not wrong.

"It's only a matter of time before the Duke or the creatures find us," Colin continues, his voice shaky. "By stealing and losing the Remedy, you sentenced us both to death."

"Charlotte said we can make it to Saint Selaphiel without it. As long as we follow the river, we'll be fine. The creatures cannot cross water, remember?"

He secures his oar, then leans in closer to me. His intensity is unnerving. This has to be part of his withdrawals.

"I know what Charlotte said, but we don't know anything about Charlotte, and we don't know anything about this river. And, by the way, I was doing fine until you, your brother, and your whole family, in fact, sucked me into your madness," he says.

Even though I would like to shrink back, I stare straight into his eyes.

"You were anything but fine," I say.

He looks like he wants to say something else, but instead, he turns and takes hold of his oars again.

I'm shaking. I don't know how to process what he said. Even though what he said was true, it doesn't feel fair. I wish Colin would stop holding my family and situations out of my control against me. He hadn't even spoken to me once in five years before this week, and now why do I expect us to suddenly be a team? How can I ever win his trust? Maybe I should just give him the Mirror. But then, I'll really have nothing.

As we continue through the labyrinth of water and wilderness, I feel lost. Tediously and silently, we row on and on until obscurity layers in over the waters. All I can hear is the oars falling into the water. Even the forest is silent around us. I wish he would say something, or I wish I knew what to say.

As we progress, we come to a part of the river with a twisting current. We are not talking, but we wordlessly steer the canoe around boulders and a rough patch. We both seem to know what we need to do and, despite everything, work well together—just like when we fought those lost people. I wish I knew how to make things right.

Colin presses ahead, seemingly nowhere near ready to stop. Maybe this is his way of processing all that he just went through. Everything around us is the same, over and over again: water and trees smothered in obscurity. We need to find shelter, though, because night has fallen—we can hardly see anything at all—and my faltering arms can't go on.

"Why don't we stop for the night?" I finally ask. "We've been going for a long time, and I haven't slept."

Through the obscurity, I can see him glare at me, as if what I said was a joke at his expense. "If we don't continue, the Duke will catch up. We aren't safe."

"Nothing can attack us on the islands. Not the creatures or the Duke," I remind him.

Colin pauses his rowing, and his hands tighten around the handle of his oar.

"Then sleep while I row." He throws some of our blankets from Charlotte on my feet, at the bottom of the canoe.

"You can't row alone."

"Give me your oar."

"What about you?"

"Later," he answers.

Even though he looks worn out, he keeps rowing. I can understand why, and I wish I could be there for him, but I'm desperate for rest. I tuck my satchel in under my head and cover myself up with the blankets he tossed my way. I curl up in the bottom of the boat, but as tired as I am, I can't rest knowing he is upset with me.

"I'm sorry," I say. "You were right. I shouldn't have left you and taken all the Remedy. Somehow, I thought that with Charlotte and the villagers, you would be fine. I never meant to cause harm or to betray you."

Colin slows his rowing and sighs. His features are still tense, but slightly more kindly. "I hope you know I care more about you than the notebook or Remedy or whatever. That's why I was upset."

I don't know why I do the next thing I do, but I sit up and come near him.

"We can't let the Duke or everything that has happened get the best of us. Think about what Charlotte said, how your father led the charge to protect the people of Saint Raphael. Colin, there is something special about you, too. You are like your father, despite everything that's happened to you. Everyone talked about how you protected those people in the forest when no other Keepers would. And even me, despite my dark family history. You still have been protecting me this whole time."

Almost immediately, he completely stops after I say that.

"But my father failed, and I don't know what to do."

I can't help but wrap my arms around him and hold him. When I do, his body relaxes and he leans into me. I close my eyes and take in the presence of him.

"You'll figure it out," I say, "and you don't have to do it alone."

He smiles.

"You'd better get some rest. I'll join you, too, pretty soon."

I let go of him and curl back up. This time, I quickly drift to sleep, the sound of Colin's rowing steadying me.

CHAPTER 20
Colin

The boat is hard to maneuver on my own, and to some extent, my mind is not working properly. I aim for the nearest island. I paddle around the whole thing to make sure it really is an island and that the creatures cannot attack us. Finally, I make it full circle. The world in this spot is thick with pine trees, except for a nook I've found. Hopefully, it will block some of the wind and shelter us from the elements.

The canoe rocks as I stand and find my footing. After I climb out, I pull the boat close to the shore and secure it to a tree in case the water levels change.

Molly is fast asleep. The space next to her is tight, but it will have to do. I settle in beside her, into her nest of blankets. My mind is spinning, but being close to Molly is calming. I press my head into her back, and my thoughts slow. I focus on her breathing, counting her breaths, and finally drift off.

In the strange place between dreams and reality, the sound of rustling near me draws my attention. A cold chill runs down my spine. Molly is supposed to be next to me, but there is only emptiness there. Did she leave, again? This is just a dream, I try to tell myself. Yet, subtle waves of movement seem to flow through the trees, and I feel watched.

"Molly?" I call out. A fire is burning near the boat on shore, but Molly isn't there.

Long shadows creep alongside me. Silhouettes and hints of dark fur move toward me—like ghosts, they are there, but not. Their bodies, neither visible nor invisible, hint at being huge, like the size of bulls. Three pairs of yellow eyes come in and out of view. My heart pounds. I have no Remedy to protect me. The eyes come closer, and in the next instant, there is a blur of teeth, sharp like shards, coming for me. The devourers of souls continue their forward charge, ready to consume me.

A loud holler comes from behind me. A fiery stick flies through the air and hits the beast's skull. The creature crumples down onto the forest floor. Molly, barely visible under her thick cloak and layers, runs up to stand between me and the beasts like a shield, hollering and waving a fiery branch at them. Finally, it slinks backwards, into the darkness of the forest.

Molly's eyes are sparkling and fierce. Her face, frosty and fearless, shines with victory.

"I'm glad I built a fire," she says.

"Thank you." I can't help but hug her.

"You would have done the same for me," she says.

Would I have? I lie down to try to go back to sleep, this time close to Molly's fire. My heartbeat steadies, and I gather my thoughts. Why didn't I think to fight them with the fire?

I don't think I can sleep, but soon enough, the frigid morning air and the brightening sky are waking me up. I realize my blankets are covered with a dusting of snow, and Molly has burrowed herself next to me, deep under my cloak and our covers. Her breathing is even and peaceful.

We slept through the whole night. I wonder how far into the day it is.

I need to relieve myself and get my bearings. I force myself away from the layers of warmth and Molly's comforting presence. As I walk into the forest, the ground and trees are covered with fresh snow. Everything is peaceful.

I find one of the tallest pines and, branch by branch, climb. When I pass the tree line, the sun is rising over the horizon. The first rays stream through crevices in the mountains and forest, and the sky transforms from a dreary gray to a pale gold.

"Colin?" Molly is awake and calling my name.

She calls again, and I begin the climb down—and almost call back out to her, but at the last moment, stop myself. She is searching between several trees—I think it's for me—but then she sits down, settling at the foot of one of them, and pulls something out of her satchel. I can't see what she's holding, but Molly deeply focuses on it, appearing to be speaking to herself at the same time.

Interacting with that something, she reminds me of my father. My body tenses and my pulse quickens. It's like I'm at the base of a dam that's about to rupture.

"What are you looking at?" I'd asked my father.

He pulled me on to his lap. "What I'm going to show you, very few people ever have seen—only the most trusted and faithful Keepers," he said.

"What is it?" My heart drummed with excitement.

"It's the Mirror of Sparrows," he'd said before showing me a little mirror with a golden frame. I remember thinking how it was smaller than what I'd expected. "It helps me make sure the people are safe."

"You watch everyone?"

"No," he laughed. "I ask to see only those who need the most help, and then, when it shows me, I know where to send guards."

"Can I see how it works?" I'd asked.

"When you make Keeper, then I can show you." My father tickled me and made me laugh, and I left the Mirror alone, though admittedly, my curiosity lingered.

I never saw the Mirror after that—that is, until right now. Molly has it. There is no doubt about it. I can no longer pretend I don't know.

CHAPTER 21
Molly

Where did Colin go? He's nowhere around our camp. This may be the perfect opportunity to finally make more use of the Mirror. I want to check up on Hugo and my mom, but most importantly, I need to find out where the Duke and his Keepers are.

I walk deeper into the woods, making sure Colin isn't near me. I find a thick tree to huddle myself against. As I pull the Mirror out, a pang of guilt tightens my stomach. Should I be sharing it with Colin? But I can't think about that now.

"Show me the Duke and how far he is," I ask the Mirror.

The glass ripples and the Duke appears before me. He and the Keepers are in the forest, walking along the banks of the river. They have big circles under their eyes like they have hardly rested. Not to mention, who knows how the Remedy is impacting them? It must be taking them significantly longer to travel by land because the Mirror shows me the length of the river and where they are in relation to Colin and me. Wait…I see Colin and—oh no.

Several birds pecking at the dirt fly away as a few branches break just beside me. I look over my shoulder, and Colin stands behind me, up against the very tree I'm resting my back on. His eyes hold mine intently. My heart sinks. I should have told him.

"What are you looking at?" he asks, staring at the Mirror in my hands.

The wind swirls the dead leaves up from the forest floor, and I wish it could take me along with it. The sinkhole of my thievery and lies has finally caved in.

He touches the frame with one finger, then pulls it away. "There once were artists," he says, unexpected emotion permeating his voice, "who put so much love into their work that it would come alive. Once, one of those artists made a special gift for the Head Keeper and his family because they were the guardians of the cities, and because they worked tirelessly to protect people." His words simmer with energy, and his eyes look brighter than I ever could have imagined.

He comes around to stand in front of me. I stare away from him, at my boots and the dirty snow. Tears threaten to well up in my eyes, but I don't let them.

"I planned to give it to Sir Jasper and the Keepers," I say. "Then, I planned on giving it to you, right after I freed Hugo. I had to help my brother. You know the Duke will kill him."

"He's probably safer than us," Colin replies, his eyes unflinchingly searching mine. "I'm pretty sure that, so long as the Duke is pursuing us, your brother is fine."

Hopefully he's right, and the Duke will leave Hugo alone so long as he's after us.

For a while, Colin stares off into the distance. I do not speak either. In the silence between us, all I feel is guilt. I've betrayed him twice since we left the city, each time over something major. I fulfilled his expectations that I was a traitor.

"The truth is, I never wanted this Mirror—only to help Hugo," I say. "Honestly, I wouldn't care if I never saw it again. I know my mother is alive, where she lives, and that she loved us, which is more of an amazing gift than anything. You can have the Mirror, but please help me rescue Hugo."

Colin sits on the ground, facing me.

"This situation will work out in our favor," Colin says. "Since we have the Mirror, we will be able to not only outmaneuver the Duke, but also help Hugo."

My hands shake as I place the Mirror in Colin's hands. "I think it might be more of a curse than a blessing."

He takes the Mirror and shakes his head. I have no idea what he is thinking, but I can't help but fold my legs in close, wrapping my arms around my knees.

"I don't think that's true. Have you used the Mirror to help us?"

I nod.

"Then it's likely the reason we are still alive."

"This Mirror destroyed both our families," I say. "But I want you to know, I never meant to be like my father."

He reaches a hand toward my face and brushes away a stray tear I hadn't even realized had been there.

"You know, I can see what Sir Jasper saw in you. My father would have seen it, too. You're not a traitor. You weren't after the Mirror in the same way as everybody else. In fact, it's amazing you found it. Do you know how many people have been searching for it? You are the one person who actually managed to figure out where it was."

"Because of my father's journal."

"Hugo couldn't figure it out. Neither could I—and I searched the whole book carefully."

These words, especially coming from Colin, take me off guard.

"Don't look at me so quizzically," he says. "Sir Jasper always saw the potential in you, and—despite my misgivings about him—I have to admit he was right."

I want to believe his words about me, but it's difficult. I need to think about everything.

"I just checked on the Duke, and he is quite far. Do you want to help me build a fire?"

He helps me to my feet, and we start gathering some wood and kindling.

Why is he so calm about everything?

CHAPTER 22
Colin

I can't believe I'm holding the Mirror. As I turn it over in my hands and in front of the crackling fire, the flames illuminate the frame of carved sparrows, branches, and leaves. It's beautiful, and I realize now how much these designs inspired my projects in Uncle Felix's old workshop. I'd seen the Mirror all those years ago. It had been such a privilege—one that marked me much more than I realized. It's a bridge to the people I miss. Touching the branches and birds of the frame makes me feel close to my father. He held this Mirror in the same way that I am.

I also see my stitches, the big circles under my eyes, and all the new bruising I've gained during this journey. My new scar, my purple and yellow skin, all the dirt, and my sunken features—not to mention facial hair—make me look ragged and tired. I've never looked worse.

"Now that you have the Mirror," Molly says, "the possibilities are limitless."

I half-smile at her. I want to be angry at her—for so many reasons—but now that I have the Mirror, I can't waste my energy that way.

She bites her lip. "What are you going to ask the Mirror first?"

That's a good question. "I'm not sure. What was your first question?"

Molly shifts and pulls her legs into herself. "I asked about my mother."

"Did it show her?"

Molly nods. "She lives in Saint Selaphiel."

"Are you going to try to see her?"

My question hit a nerve because she doesn't answer right away.

"I'm not sure if she would want to see me." When she says that, I can feel the weight of her fears in the quietness of her voice.

Molly stands. "If you don't mind, I'm going to go for a little walk. I'm sure you have lots of questions for the Mirror, and you might be better off doing that on your own."

"I don't mind." I want to say, it's not like you ever asked for my approval before. "But I'm here if you need me."

Molly's eyes linger on mine. She's considering what I said, but I don't think she believes my words because she eases away from me and walks off into the forest.

Being alone with the Mirror is strange. I'm not sure what to ask it. There are too many possibilities. I wish she had stayed.

I close my eyes and think. Then, I remember what my father would always ask first.

"Please show me the most important thing I need to know," I ask the Mirror.

The glass in the Mirror looks like it's rippling, and a scene shifts into clarity. My father is there, right before me—just how I remember him. My throat clenches. What is the Mirror going to show me?

He is in our old home, in his office, working at his desk. It must be late because it's night outside his window, and the candles are lit. It feels like I'm right there. Then, the bell at the front door rings, and my father stands up. The image follows him to the front door. When he opens up, two men step in—Molly's father and the Duke. My father welcomes them into his office.

"You know why we are here," the Duke tells my father. He proceeds to demand the Mirror, claiming it should belong to the public, not only one family, but my father refuses. Before I know it, the Duke is shouting at my father, and Molly's father is attempting to calm the situation.

"I know what you did," my father says to the Duke. Based on what Charlotte said, my father must be referring to Saint Raphael.

The conflict escalates, and my whole body tenses. A brutal scene unfolds before me. The Duke makes a stab at my father. The man I love and miss doubles over, and his body falls to the ground.

"You forced me to do this," the Duke shouts, and he stabs again. Molly's father tries to stop him, but the Duke shoves him away with such force that he lands against my father's desk. There, Sir Fitzpatrick's eyes catch sight of a box on the work surface.

My mother walks in next.

"What's going on in here?" she asks. My whole body feels like it is crumpling, but I cannot take my eyes off the images. She barely has the chance to take in the room before the Duke lunges at her. She screams. With his last bit of strength, my father tries to help her, but he doesn't succeed. The Duke is too strong. My mother collapses to the ground, knocking over a set of crystal vases as she falls. Glass shatters everywhere.

While the Duke is preoccupied with my mother, Sir Fitzpatrick slides the box off my father's desk and slips away. When the Duke realizes what happened, he runs after him.

For so long, I thought of the Duke as my family—the one person who was there for me—but it was all a lie. He pretended to be my friend, like my father even, when all along he was the one who had killed my parents. And after Molly's father escaped with the Mirror, the Duke dealt with it by blaming him for my parents' murder.

I close my eyes and steady myself, but a new image begins—not in the Mirror, but in my mind's eye. I'm alone in my father's office, walking across the shards of glass and the blood, towards my parents' bodies lying on the ground. Next, there is the pounding at the door: the Duke. He's come to help me. But how had he known I needed help?

I push my hands through my hair, as if I could wipe away all the images replaying in my thoughts. I don't think I can handle this. The forest around me seems to twist and contort. It spins around me. Images of my parents continue to flood my mind, and resentment ignites into anger in my heart, like a smoldering fire. I was such a fool, and I hate myself for it.

I wish I had more Remedy, even just a little bit.

I pick up branches from the ground, throw them on to the fire, and pace.

The Duke has betrayed me, over and over again, and I just followed him like a lost puppy.

I find more dry wood to add to the fire. I can't see straight or think straight except for the flames.

"Why?" I shout. Tears are streaming down my face, and all I can do is toss more branches onto the fire. As the flames and smoke leap higher, I add on more branches. I want to burn all my past mistakes away. I want to burn my stupidity away. Every time I throw a stick into the fire, it's like I'm throwing one more dumb decision away to be consumed and done away with.

The fire is increasing, but it's not until its flames rise taller than me that I realize how out of control it has become. The smoke and the heat are suffocating. I need water. I need to stop this. Where is Molly?

I lower my knees to the forest floor, and push my hands into the dirt and remnants of snow. After I dig into the ground, I throw handful after handful of dirt and snow onto the fire. Soon, I realize, more dirt and snow are being thrown on, but not only by me.

"Molly?" My voice breaks when I say her name. She's back, helping me extinguish the flames. We continue to throw earth and snow onto the fire until, finally, we are able to contain it.

Soil, dirt, and smoke cover us. Charred wood lies all around. Everything is quiet. She is quiet.

Molly places a gentle hand on my shoulder, and I lean over and push my head into her. Tears roll down my face again. Her fingers touch against my cheek.

"What happened?" she asks.

Where do I even start?

"The Duke killed my parents—not your father." I fix my eye back on hers.

Her face pales.

As I look at her, and the charred remnants of all the branches behind her, my heart steadies. The Mirror showed me this, out of everything, for a reason. I need to be smart about this.

"I can't run away from him anymore. I have to make him pay for everything he did. I can't be the person I used to be. I can't let him get away with this."

She shifts her eyes away from mine.

"What do you mean?"

I take hold of her shoulders. I want her to understand me. "We have the Mirror. We can do anything."

"Are you going to try to kill him?" she asks, her face all creased up.

"After everything he did, we need everyone to know who he is. We need to pull him apart, piece by piece."

Her eyes shine with what I think might be tears.

"Are you crying?" I ask.

Her muscles tighten. "Just don't turn into him," she says.

Does she really think I would ever become like him?

I let go of her and hold the Mirror up again. "Show me the Duke," I say. "What is he doing now and where is he?"

The Mirror ripples. The Duke is flipping through the notebook and pulling out its pages, laying pieces of it together, creating some sort of tree.

"That's the map that led me to the Mirror," Molly says.

"I wonder if he's going to figure out we already have it. He sees you've unsewn the pages of the book, and he knows we've not only been surviving the wilderness, but that we found that hidden village."

"I'm glad the Mirror showed me what it did." I tuck it away. "Now, I can fight back. I wanted to before, but I was unsure of myself. Nothing can stand in my way from this point forward."

CHAPTER 23
Molly

"Let's stay here tonight," Colin says.

He has been obsessively watching the Duke in the Mirror—all day. I'm upset, too—after all, that man destroyed my family—but I don't want to risk my life with scheming and revenge.

"Even with the Mirror, it would be better if we kept moving." I want to be supportive, but Colin is overestimating what the Mirror can do.

"We are the ones the Duke should be afraid of," Colin says.

"Well, I need to do something. Do you mind if I take a look?" I ask. He needs a break. Maybe he can think a little more clearly this way.

He hands it to me. "You want to check on the Duke?"

"No. I trust you with that." I turn my attention to the Mirror. "Where can Colin and I find food?"

Colin moves closer so he can see. "Good idea."

The image changes to that of a pheasant snug on the ground. I smile.

"Can I use your knife?" I ask, and he hands it to me.

We follow the Mirror's directions into the forest. When the pheasant comes into sight, I unsheathe Colin's blade, readying myself to throw it. Just as I lift my arm, Colin places a hand on the small of my back. His unexpected touch startles me. I would have been fine throwing the knife before, but now, my hand is wobbly. I steady myself, remembering what Sir Jasper said: *focus*.

My blade flies fast.

The pheasant flaps its wings to try to escape. It rises a few wingbeats and falls.

"Can you help me prepare it?" I ask.

"Let's go cook our dinner." Colin is smiling for the first time today.

We find the pheasant in the brambles and walk back to our makeshift little camp. While I build a fire, he guts the bird and plucks its feathers, then we set the meat to roast over the bed of flames.

"Since I've been watching the Duke," Colin says, "I noticed he's been looking at how you pulled apart the notebook. I think he senses you found the Mirror. If I'm correct, he'll be more ruthless than ever. We need to deal with him right away."

"Maybe we should just make it to Saint Selaphiel and find the Ruler. She can help protect us and the cities."

"Taking care of the Duke is protecting us and the cities," he says, cutting off a large hunk of the meat and handing it to me. "We can't count on anybody but ourselves. You know that."

Hungry, I take a big bite. It's very tasty—maybe some of the best food I've ever had.

"Colin, can I be honest with you?"

"That would be nice, for a change."

I can't help but squirm, but I earned that.

"Don't let the Mirror take over your life. My family was destroyed because of my father's obsession with the Mirror. There are people who can help us. We don't have to do this alone."

"You don't think I've had any experience with a parent obsessed with the Mirror? Besides, your father didn't do anything wrong, and we do have to do this alone."

I shake my head. "My father might not have killed your parents, but he was greedy for the Mirror, and that destroyed our family. It was Sir Jasper who was there to help us when he wasn't."

"It was not your father that destroyed your family. It was the Duke. He was the one responsible." Colin fiddles with some leaves and twigs on the ground. "I have always been curious about you, even with everything that happened between our families."

"You can ask me anything," I say.

He picks up the Mirror, but his eyes are on me, not the glass. "Is Molly trustworthy, and how does she feel about me?" he asks.

I swallow hard, and my heart tightens. I thought he would have been asking me, not the Mirror. And right in front of me? Already the image in the Mirror is rippling. It shows me bringing him and his Uncle Felix bread, me arguing with Hugo, then praying and trying to figure out what to do about the Mirror. Next, it shows me looking at him at the contender testing and Sir Jasper urging me to learn how to focus.

"Interesting," Colin says.

Blood rushes to my face. I can't believe he is seeing all this.

The Mirror continues and shows us in the wilderness, helping each other survive. I guess the Mirror is showing I am trustworthy, and the tightness of built-up anxiety begins to loosen.

I motion for him to hand me the Mirror. "My turn," I say.

He leans his head in toward me, his eyes piercing, but he hands me the Mirror.

"Is Colin trustworthy?" I ask the glass.

The Mirror shows me images of Colin studying and training. The Duke is always there, spewing fear into his mind, and the work he makes Colin do is exceedingly intense—insane, even. Then, the Mirror switches to the image of Colin's anguished face when he sees what the Duke did to his parents. I can't imagine what he must be feeling right now, seeing all this.

The image ripples once more, to the two of us in the river, surviving together, and in the forest, asleep in the canoe, Colin a protective cocoon of warmth.

According to the Mirror, Colin is a mix of ruthlessness and tenderness. My heart is heavy for him.

"I guess we can trust each other," Colin says.

After we finish the food and ready ourselves to settle down for the night, we lie down beside the fire. I need his warmth, too, but am cautious about being too close.

I gaze up at the night sky, at the thousands upon thousands of stars above us. I even see a slew of shooting stars. Colin isn't looking at the Mirror anymore, but up at the sky with me.

"They are amazing, aren't they?" I ask.

"They are." He takes hold of my hand.

At first I'm not sure about it, but then I feel like we are going to be all right—just like when we jumped into the river. And maybe Colin won't be so obsessed with the Duke anymore.

For the first time in days, I feel safe and begin to finally relax, my eyes heavy with fatigue.

CHAPTER 24
Colin

I run my fingers through Molly's tangled hair as she falls asleep. Her breathing is steadying. I pushed things too far with the Mirror, but it worked out. When she finds out I carried out my plans for revenge, she'll be upset. But I have to resolve matters with the Duke once and for all. It's to protect us. We deserve peace. Not only did he kill my family and poison every aspect of my life, he destroyed hers, too.

He caused me to love him even though he was my parents' murderer. I feel sick and ashamed about who I've been. My gullibility and neediness opened the door to the Duke's manipulations, and never again will I blindly trust someone—nor will I have to, thanks to the Mirror.

I lay an additional blanket over Molly and turn my attention back to the Mirror.

"Show me the Duke again," I ask.

The image ripples, and the Mirror shows me the Keepers and the Duke are in the forest over the water. By their fire, some sit around in drunken laughter, while others snore. Their ruthless faces, however, are forever etched in my mind.

"Where is the Remedy?" I ask the Mirror.

The Mirror shows me a leather satchel sitting just besides the Duke, his hand draped over it. He rests slumped against a tree, drooping to one side. Without their precious supply of Remedy, the Keepers' and Duke's souls will be fair game for the creatures' appetites—unless they can fight the way they are supposed to, with fire.

After making sure our fire is well fed and secured within a ring of large stones, I pull the canoe into the river. The boat scratches against the mud and the rocks. I hope this doesn't wake Molly up. I glance one more time toward her, but she doesn't stir.

The surface of the water barely ripples as my canoe moves ahead. Darkness and the forest engulf me and no reflections appear around me. The stars and moon must be hidden by clouds now because it's like I'm moving through an empty abyss. Only the shadow of the forest looms ahead, and even if I can't see them, the creatures are watching me. But I have the Mirror.

What Molly and Charlotte didn't realize, and what no one else but my family knew, is that the Mirror protects against the creatures. The Mirror, my father told me, creates a shield around those who carry it. That's most likely the main reason Molly has been able to survive, besides the water and reindeer.

The bottom of the boat pushes over something hard. I've arrived at the bank. As I step on to the twisting root-filled ground, it is difficult to hoist the boat higher.

My heart tightens. In the midst of the dense obscurity, glints of hungry eyes, snarls, and shard-like teeth menace, but they will not attack me. I pull out the Mirror, as if to show them, and to re-orient myself.

The Duke and his guards are a ways off, all of them drifting to sleep now. While I know the Keepers' fatigue and alcohol will help conceal my arrival, what if I am caught? All would be lost, and the Duke would have the Mirror. But I also couldn't have left the Mirror behind. I need it for protection and guidance.

The deeper I push through the trees, the more the forest seems to press against me. Each of my steps seems to crunch too loud. Will they hear me?

I approach the nook where the Keepers have set up camp. Their occasional snores and the crackle of the campfire fill the night. The Duke lies nearby, his hand still covering the satchel. Hopefully, he'll be too asleep to notice as I slide the precious stash away from him.

The leather bag is heavier than I would have expected, and it's dragging against the dirt and leaves. The sound of it is unnerving, but I cannot lift it off the ground. As I move the satchel, the Duke's hand is still on it, his arm extending as I pull. My hand is shaking, but it's too late to turn back now. I pause. What will happen when I take the satchel and his hand drops?

I take a deep breath and tilt the bag, lowering the Duke's hand to the ground. At long last, I am able to remove it. The Duke stirs, adjusting his position, but settles back down. He doesn't realize the satchel is gone. I hoist the load of Remedy over my shoulder and rush away, behind a nearby tree. The coolness of the bark helps me to steady myself.

I glance back one more time. The Duke is peaceful and fast asleep—not for long. When he wakes up to face the creatures, he will realize I'm not the pawn he thought I was. He will regret everything he did to me and my family.

CHAPTER 25
Molly

Despite my blanket and cloak, cold permeates to my bones. In vain, I curl into myself for more warmth. I'm shivering and can't sleep. I reach for Colin, but he is no longer beside me—only emptiness. Wasn't he lying right beside me when I fell asleep? Finally, I open my eyes and wake up to silence and stillness. As I take in my surroundings, I realize the Mirror is gone, too.

I squint my eyes to see into the forest and listen, but the woods are freezing and still. Colin is nowhere near. How long has he been gone? After some time, the sound of rowing breaks through the quiet. My heart sinks. I should have noticed the canoe was missing. I bury myself back down under the covers and pretend to be fast asleep.

After Colin has paddled in, he walks over to where I am sleeping and checks on me. I wonder if he can tell I'm awake. I guess not, because he fiddles about, adding wood to the fire, and settles himself back down beside me. His breathing slows, and it's not long before he is asleep again.

Adrenaline courses through me as I slip out from under my covers and try to piece together what Colin has been up to. He has a new bag—and by the slain dragon emblem, it's a Keeper satchel. When I open it up, I find not only the Mirror, but an enormous number of vials of Remedy.

I pull the Mirror out and sit with it by the edge of the river.

"Where was Colin?" I whisper.

The image in the glass ripples to Colin among the Duke's guards. He is almost imperceptible in the way he slinks behind the trees, and even with the Mirror, I have trouble distinguishing him. Like a shadow, he stalks around them and slides away the satchel sitting beside the Duke. *He stole all their Remedy.*

I can't believe he is feeding the Keepers' and the Duke's souls to the creatures. True, they have acted despicably, and they should know how to fight the creatures with fire, but do they deserve *this*? It's too much.

When I consider how the Duke and those guards treated us, as well as the constant fleeing for our lives, I'm tempted to let them reap Colin's wrath. I despise them for having tortured us and our loved ones—but can I let Colin do this? The reality is, exacting revenge on the Duke and his men this way will destroy *him*. He doesn't understand the life of a murderer—what it's like to be a traitor and to have the weight of wrongful death plague you wherever you go, whatever you do. The other issue is, if he has this much Remedy at his disposal, won't he end up using it? That poison will kill him. If I let him hold on to this much of it, what kind of a friend am I?

But would Colin ever forgive me for interfering? No matter how he feels, I care too much about him to let him ruin his life.

As I sit here trying to figure out what to do, only one viable solution comes to mind—and it's risky. I need to return the Remedy to the Keepers. He's going to be angry, and the Duke will be after us still, but it is the only adequate choice. What else am I supposed to do, let Colin keep all of the vials and let the Duke and his guards be condemned to insanity?

I pace along the bank of the river in the same way that so many questions are running through my thoughts.

In order to execute my plan, how will I stay safe? Can I carry fire the whole way? I wonder how Colin managed.

"How did Colin make it to the Duke safely," I ask the Mirror.

The glass in the Mirror ripples and shows me an image of itself.

Strange.

"What does that mean?" I ask.

It's hard for me to understand what the Mirror shows me next, except the glass ripples to an image of me holding the Mirror, and a bright glow of light surrounds me.

Could it be that the Mirror is like a shield? I think that's what I am seeing.

In as complete of silence as possible I return to where Colin is asleep and lift the stolen satchel. It's heavy, and the bottles clink together.

Colin stirs.

What if he wakes up? I break out into a cold sweat.

But his breathing settles again and even deepens.

As I paddle the boat across the water, I remember the last time I left Colin behind and was crossing water. It did not end well. Except this time, there is no fog. Instead, snow begins to fall—not just a little, but thick sheets of it.

I hope I'm not making a mistake. Because it is beautiful and peaceful, my mind stops racing. I lift my face up to the sky and let the flakes drift on to my cheeks and nose. Somehow, maybe everything will work out fine.

Before long, a nook in the root covered bank of the river welcomes me in. Once the canoe and oars are secure, I pull out the Mirror once more and make sure I'm heading in the correct direction. I don't mind the obscurity because my eyes have adjusted, and the light of the moon through the trees and reflecting off the beginning layers of snow is quite enough to make my way. The reality is, there is barely any night left, and the darkness is my friend. I have just a short while to drop off the satchel and make it back.

When I come to the Duke's camp, his Keepers are still fast asleep, without any awareness of the harm that was about to befall them—and they will never know I saved their lives, perhaps at the very expense of my own and Colin's.

I need to hurry. The worst that could happen now is for them to wake up and find me with the Mirror. The weight of the danger of hits me. Cold sweat trickles down my back. *What am I doing?*

I place the bag of Remedy at the edge of the camp—as close to the Duke as possible—and run back toward the canoe and the river. As I do, the day begins to replace the night. There is a good chance Colin will be awake by the time I make it back. As I cross the water, I'm scared about how he will react. At least Colin won't have the blood of murder on his hands. But if the Duke and his guards catch us, maybe I will.

Chapter 26
Colin

I'm covered with snow, as if I'm part of the ground. Not only that, the fire has gone out. I push myself up, shake the powdery ice from on top of me, and move to where the fire is supposed to be burning warm. Where is Molly? There are no traces of her, not a footprint in the snow, and where she was asleep, an undisturbed blanket of white. My satchel with the Remedy and Mirror are gone, too.

My breathing becomes heavy, and my head begins to spin. I search through the blankets where we were sleeping and glance around everywhere. She also took the canoe. Could she have taken everything?

The Mirror said I could trust her. None of this makes sense. I thought today was going to be a new, happy day. Instead, everything is wrong.

I busy myself with the fire. Rebuilding it is more difficult than I anticipated. Not only am I suddenly recollecting yesterday's out-of-control blaze, but the surface of all the wood is damp. Somehow, I find a few combustible pieces sheltered beneath some of the other logs, but my hands shake as I pull together the kindling—from cold, anger, fear, maybe even Remedy withdrawals. Maybe all of those at once.

Finally, the flames take.

As I warm my hands, a movement on the river, a shadow gliding across the surface of the water, catches my eye. Molly is rowing back to our camp. A mix of anger, relief, and curiosity battle for priority within me.

When she reaches the shore, I leave the fire and help hoist the boat in. When we're done stowing the oars, we sit and warm ourselves by the little fire. I'm hoping she'll volunteer information, but instead, we sit in awkward silence.

"Where did you go?" I ask.

She pulls out the Mirror and places it beside my feet. It sinks down, half-buried in the snow. I pick it up and dust it off.

"Show me where Molly was," I say.

The glass ripples and reveals Molly walking through the forest, heading toward the Keepers, holding the satchel of Remedy. After she places the bag near the Duke, she runs back to our canoe. Little does she realize, she's leaving tracks in the snow, leading straight back to where she left the boat. Since it started snowing while she was traveling there—maybe she didn't realize. I keep watching, hoping that somehow what I'm seeing is mistaken; that somehow, this situation is not as it seems. Yet, according to the Mirror, she did return the Remedy to the Duke and his Keepers.

I can't help but stand and start collecting our belongings, unable to think of anything else except to leave, fast. Doesn't she realize our very lives are on the line?

"Why?" I ask.

Her face is tense with fear. "I didn't want you to be forever burdened with those men's fates."

"The Duke and his guards could be on your trail right now. We could have been free," I say as I pack. "We could have lived without ever worrying about the Duke again. Now, they'll keep coming after us, and we may never have a chance like this again."

"Is this really only about our safety?"

"Think about everything he did to both our families!" My voice is shaking. "Think about what they did! This was what they deserved, and our freedom is what we deserve."

"We still have the Mirror," she says. "With it, we will be able to make it to Saint Selaphiel. All we have to do is make it to the city, and then we can fight for proper justice with the Ruler and Sir Jasper."

"That's not true. The Duke has the Ruler wrapped around his little finger. Trust me. I know. Besides, we're exhausted. They have horses. We have no food. They have heaps of supplies. They have every advantage over us, even if we do have the Mirror. By saving them, you've condemned us. The Duke won't stop until he's caught us. Don't you see what he's already done and how much worse it can get? And not to mention, he must know we have the Mirror. How else could we have found them? That was stupid of you, Molly."

She glares at me. "I don't expect you to agree with my decision, but I believe what I did was right." Her voice is quivering.

"You think you are doing good, but you are not," I snap and throw our belongings into the boat. "Can you stomp the fire out? We have to go."

She mumbles something to herself says as she throws dirt and snow over the fire, and only icy cold air remains. It hurts because truthfully, she was the one person I believed was true, and I don't want to lose her. But I can't stay with her if she's going to be this unpredictable.

"Let's hurry," I say.

"Don't you want to at least check the Mirror before we rush off?"

I pick up my set of oars. "We can do that on the go," I say.

With a sour look on her face, she steps into the canoe, and I push us back into the river. Because of Molly, we'll be rowing for our lives again, who knows for how long? I'm so tired of all this fleeing.

Molly pulls the Mirror out of her satchel and asks it for information about where we are.

"We're about a day away from Saint Selaphiel."

"I know that already. What about the Duke?" As my muscles ache from the renewed paddling, the fact that she just saved the very people who are hunting us baffles me. "Don't you believe the cities would be safer without them?" I ask.

"But you had condemned them to perpetual madness. That's the kind of decision the Duke would make. You're better than that."

I shake my head. "This was different. I was keeping people safe, us among them."

"We can tell Sir Jasper." Her voice tightens. "I am going to explain to him the truth about everything."

"What's he going to do about it?" Even as I say the words, I remember Sir Jasper is the one who saved my life in the wilderness.

"Sir Jasper was the one who tried to protect my parents against the Duke when everyone else condemned them. He was the one who looked after Hugo and me even after our own mother left us."

"Do you think he knew the Duke was the one responsible for the death of my parents?" I pause. "Because he certainly didn't help me."

Her eyes lock on mine for an extended moment. "I don't know."

She holds up the Mirror and angles it toward me. "Show us the Duke." The glass shows the Duke packing up.

"He is flustered," I say. "Look. He's realized the bag of Remedy moved."

"They were up so late drinking, they don't even have their act together. He probably thinks one of the Keepers moved it because snow has fallen over most of my footsteps." Molly has a glint in her eyes.

"Maybe," I say.

Molly raises the Mirror again. "Show me Hugo." By the sad expression on her face, he isn't well. "Someone needs to do something for him. I wish Sir Jasper could check up on him," she says.

"Sir Jasper will be riding on the road to Saint Selaphiel with the returning caravan of provisions and the Ruler. They should reach the city around the same time as us."

"I forgot the caravan would be returning after the Keeper contests. I wonder who made Keeper."

"Who cares? And by the way, please don't tell Sir Jasper about the Mirror if we make it to the city."

Molly's brow creases. "Why not?"

"We don't need more complications."

"Part of me wonders about his glasses," she says.

"His glasses? The ones with all those gems around the rims? Why?"

"When he uses them, I think he sees more than what meets the eye. I think he'll find out about the Mirror whether we want him to or not."

Could she be right?

"Can you row? We need to find out in the Mirror."

After we trade jobs, I ask, "What do Sir Jasper's glasses do?"

Two images appear at once: one with Sir Jasper wearing the glasses, the other with images around the people he is conversing with.

"You see?" Molly says.

I nod.

The snow begins falling again, covering our head and shoulders, and its quietness commands a strange peace. With her rosy cheeks and a glimmer in her eyes, Molly seems carefree despite our predicament—it makes no sense to me. We keep rowing together in silence, but I wonder if our paths should diverge.

"Listen, go to Sir Jasper if you want to," I tell her. "But I need to take care of the Duke my way, once and for all."

She sighs and climbs over to be next to me. We paddle side by side. It's not the most efficient, but the warmth of her presence is comforting in the cold. It's funny how we can be together, yet so apart in our thinking and already on different courses.

Suddenly, my eyes catch sight of reindeer, a whole herd of them. They seem to be tracking us along the bank.

Molly's eyes, wide in astonishment, meet mine. "They're protecting us," she says, breathless, "just like on the island."

She stops paddling and rests her head on my shoulder. I close my eyes and press my head against hers. I wish I could pretend that all is fine, like her, but I cannot.

"We have to keep going, Molly," I finally say and pick my oar back up.

Chapter 27
Molly

The cold air bites at my face, burns my lungs, and whips my chestnut strands into icy snarls. The gray sky weighs on me, and the frost-covered branches, too. Except, from the banks of the river, the reindeer follow us constantly now. The beating of their hooves joins into a rhythm with our rowing, strengthening me against all logic.

This whole predicament is my fault: we are rushing to Saint Selaphiel, now, and since the Duke and his Keepers are on horseback, they could possibly arrive before us and catch us at the wall. What if he somehow arrives to the gates first? We will never be able to enter into the city, then.

Unfortunately, I can't help but wonder if, even if by some miracle we do make it into the city, Colin and I will ever see each other again. Will he pretend I don't exist, like he did before? And when he takes the Mirror—since it was his father's—what will I be left with?

Hopefully I can find Sir Jasper, and then, I hope to find my mother's place. The image of her purple door on Crumb Street is constantly on my mind.

I've tried to recollect the last time we saw each other, but it's like piecing together shredded petals of a torn flower. The only details that come to mind are the Keepers showing up at our home and demanding my father. My mother was crying. That's the last I remember of her. But I need to find my mother, even though she never came to find us.

As I row, my thoughts drift to the past. My next memory, after that incident, is waking up under a pile of blankets next to Hugo.

"Good evening," an older woman, her gray hair twisted into a loose bun, said as she stoked a fire near me. Yellowing and peeling flower-patterned paper lined the walls of the smallish room, and a musty old rug, the floor. Beside the kitchen wares and the mat and covers Hugo and I were lying on, there wasn't much else to see.

"Where are we?" I pulled myself up and asked. Hugo was still curled up next to me under the blanket.

"You're safe," the woman answered.

The Keepers had taken our father, but where was our mother?

"Where is my mom?" I asked.

The woman shrugged. "I'm only following Keepers' orders. It's the Keepers who'll be taking care of the two of you from now on, not your parents."

I nudged Hugo awake, holding his hand tight, and he finally stirred.

"We only have each other now," I whispered to him.

"Eat." The woman handed me and Hugo each a bowl of soup. "Who knows what the days ahead hold for the two of you, given your circumstances."

"Will the Keepers really help us?" I asked.

Hugo shot me an irritated glare.

The woman nodded. "Some of them are for you."

"Who?" Hugo asked.

"Sir Jasper, for one," the lady said. "Not sure how he plans to handle you both, though."

Just then, a cart's wheels could be heard stopping outside the door, and a burly man with a cap and thick black beard opened the door. He waddled inside, warmed his hands by the fire, and drank a bowl of soup.

"You can have another chance to see your father," he said. "But we don't have to go if you don't want to. It's not gonna be pretty."

"Why would you even offer?" the lady contested.

"Let them decide," he answered.

"They're too young. How are they supposed to know?"

"Let them," he repeated himself and turned his attention to Hugo and me.

The two of us squeezed each other's hands under the blankets. We had both known we wanted to see our father one more time, no matter the cost, and we followed the man without any question. He gave us thick wool sweaters to pull on, and we curled up under several blankets in the back of his cart. He also gave us a loaf of bread to nibble on.

After what felt like an eternity of bumpy hours, the cart stopped. The smell of salt permeated the air and the sound of crashing waves echoed below us. This was our first time being near the sea.

"Don't make any mischief," the man had warned us. "You don't want to draw any more trouble to yourselves than you already have."

Quite a number of people had been there, including Colin, I remember. Still, all else was a bit of a blur, except that a group of men walked up toward us and took us to a hooded man in chains. Then, our father was pulled out from under his covering. I remember hands directing Hugo and me to him. He hugged us and kissed the top of our heads as best he could.

We said our goodbyes, then made our way back to the cart. Then, all became quiet, except for the creaking of the wood in the carts and the horses and the pounding of the sea. Someone, maybe the Duke, listed the charges against him.

"Close your eyes now," the man had said. "It's no good for you to be watching this part." I did close my eyes, and Hugo and I held on to each other, but I still heard the orders to drop my father over the edge, and then the sound of chains clattering, and then silence.

The man tried to comfort us as best as he could. "We'll arrive at your new home by sunrise. Just try to rest."

I tried to sleep, but I kept hearing my father's chains.

While continuing to pull my oars through the water below, I try to hold my tears back. The reality of my loneliness is sinking in, but just when I don't think I can handle much more of my thoughts, I realize night has fallen and that the city walls—the tops of which are lined by torches of fire—appear in the distance. We have made it to Saint Selaphiel.

The river is bringing us as far as we can go, and the bridge that presumably leads to the main road and the gates is just ahead of us.

Colin pulls the Mirror out. "Where is the Duke?" he asks.

The glass ripples. The Duke and his Keepers are making their way toward the gate, but they are held back because of the length of the caravan, which itself is led by Sir Jasper.

"Show us the city gate," Colin tells the Mirror, fidgeting with its corners.

The Mirror shows us Sir Jasper is already approaching the guards at the gates.

"They'll be searching for creatures, not us," Colin says. "If we hurry up, we might have a shot at smuggling ourselves into the city with them. We should split up to better conceal ourselves."

He makes it sound so easy. I'm guessing that will be the end of our teamwork.

After we tuck our boat under the bridge, Colin stands next to me in silence. We stand this way several moments, then he bounds out of the canoe, leaving everything behind except the Mirror and without saying a thing.

Abruptly, I'm alone.

That's all? Not even a goodbye after everything we just went through? It's like we just went back to how everything was between us before, during our five years of silence.

I sit down in the canoe, and take everything in. The oars Colin and I couldn't wait to be done with, the blankets folded up at the bottom that we slept under, the etchings on the hull that Colin admired so much. How can everything feel so hollow this fast?

At the sound of the caravan's wheels rolling on the road above me, my thoughts begin to refocus on the matter at hand: entering into the city undetected and finding my mother. This isn't a good time for me to be sad. I have to move efficiently and be smart if I'm going to evade the Duke and his Keepers. Good thing I've had lots

of practice hiding and concealing myself and overcoming
loneliness.

CHAPTER 28
Colin

I'm sorry I had to leave Molly behind, but if I'm going to be able to hold the Duke accountable, it was necessary. Everyone in the caravan seems familiar with each other, but I'm hoping that, as we approach the city, people will be too distracted and excited to notice me. I find a cluster of people walking behind a cart loaded with barrels of what looks like apple cider. Though at first they give me strange looks—probably because I'm filthy—they soon keep walking and ignore me.

A handful of Keepers watch everyone entering through the first gate leading into the outer wall. Thankfully, I make my way with the caravan through that first wall. Next, we travel across the fields and orchards to the second, inner wall. That's where most of the Keepers are stationed. Sir Jasper will be there, and he is not easily fooled.

And indeed, as we approach, Sir Jasper and his Keepers have traveled ahead and are there, supervising the caravan's entry into the city, watching the incoming crowd, interrogating each person as they enter. The Duke must be really close, too. Though it would be unreasonable for the Saint Selaphiel guards to know who I am, Sir Jasper's Keepers could readily recognize me. With the dirt, my facial hair, and new scar, I hope I'm well concealed, but for good measure, I bundle my face in a scarf, too.

As I approach the gate, I head toward one of the Saint Selaphiel guards. He squints his eyes at me like I'm odd.

"What's your purpose here?" the guard asks.

"Pilgrimage and prayer at the Hall of Prayers." When I had asked the Mirror where to go, that was the place it showed me. It was also where my father used to stay when he came to this city, and I remember going there with him once, when I was small.

"Last name?"

"Thompson."

Instead of writing this information in his register, he continues to stare at me.

"Remove your hood and step aside please," he says.

Right then, Sir Jasper glances my way. He puts on his glasses, the ones Molly was so adamant about. My heart sinks. Over the guard's shoulder, I can see the city's streets, but my chances of making a run for it are not good.

"Where will you be staying, again?" the guard asks me.

My throat clenches. "The Hall of Prayers," I manage to say. I glance back at Sir Jasper. I know he sees me, because he is still staring at me, and I swear by the knowing look in his eye that he recognizes me.

"Why are you so dirty?" the guard asks. "No other member of the caravan has this much dirt on them."

"I fell into a ditch on my way," I say.

The guard rolls his eyes, then looks back at Sir Jasper for directives. The latter nods, and the guard motions for me to move on. "But clean yourself up. We don't want any vagrants in our city."

As I step through to the other side of the gate, my heart pounds like it's about to explode. Why did Sir Jasper not stop me? My guess is he is protecting me from the Duke.

Inside the city, despite the cold and the late evening hour, all the shops are open and light up the streets. The road is covered with gray slush and a surprising number of people milling around. After so much time in the wilderness, the lights, smells, and people are almost overwhelming.

I stop by one of the store's displays. In it sit several hundred different metal trinkets and contraptions. I'm tempted to enter inside to look at some of their mechanisms, but then I see my reflection in the display window. Lost among the items, my face stares back at me.

No wonder the guard was disturbed about my appearance. I probably smell, too. While I have seen myself in the Mirror, this is different. In the Mirror, the image always fades to something else. Now, my face stays, and I am filthy. Not just the kind of dirt that can be washed away with water, but the kind that is part of who I am. I helped the Duke perpetrate his wrongdoings. The prestige the Duke gave me blinded me from truth and from who I was becoming: power hungry, just like him. I, in fact, obstructed justice for my father, and, if I think about it, by my prejudice and ignorance, was complicit in all the people the Duke killed or went after, including Molly's father.

Suddenly, I feel bad about leaving Molly. Even though it would have been difficult and too conspicuous for us to enter the city together, leaving her like that was wrong.

I take a long look at where Molly stitched me up. Her work is tidy, but this scar will never let me forget about her. In truth, I miss her. It would have been fun to wander through these neighborhoods together and have a proper meal.

As I walk the slushy, snowy streets toward the Hall of Prayers, some of the people passing by give me funny looks, and I don't blame them.

After I have long since stopped feeling my toes, the Hall of Prayers and its adjoining cathedral, the Cathedral of Saint Selaphiel, are at the top of the street ahead. The buildings are tall, the highest at least three stories high with portions of intricate facades and stained-glass windows.

As I come close, the wind swirling around pleasantly lifts flurries of leaves and snowflakes, as if to greet me. At the entry, I try to open the doors, but they are locked. Though I knock, no one answers. Have I arrived too late in the evening?

In the wood of the main doorway, an artist has carved intricate patterns of flowers, berries, and leaves. I run my fingers over them. They remind me of the designs carved into the canoe. I wish for some how, some way, to go in.

Finally, I try to knock again, and beg. "Please, let me in." I've never heard my voice like that before. In it, I hear my own longing for rest.

An attention-seeking cough catches my ear, and I turn to face a strangely familiar older man sitting on a mat, leaning up against the wall. Where do I know him from? His white hair is unusually big and fluffy, same as his white beard. He's carving a piece of wood with a sharp, well-honed knife, and the shavings gently drift on to the ground below him. I wish I could place him.

"And here I'd heard you were good at unlocking doors," he says.

Does he know who I am, and if so, how? I adjust the hood around my face.

"Arrived with the caravan?" he asks, motioning me with his knife to approach.

I move toward him in slow, cautious steps. His eyes squint at me, causing my blood to pulse.

"I remember you from when you were just a tot," he exclaims and laughs. "Well, look at you now."

Something tells me this man, though he looks strange and out of place, is of special significance to me.

"Do you remember me?" he asks.

I shake my head no.

"I'm the Whittler," he says. "You used to always ask me questions. Come, sit down with me."

At first, I don't want to. We're really going to look like two vagrants, and there is so much I need to do, most important of which is finding shelter.

"Don't worry. I won't harm you," he says.

Something about this man tugs at me, and I sit beside him.

He smiles, but his eyes are actually tearing up. He puts a hand on my shoulder. "I'm glad you are here," he says. "I'll have to put you in the common room, though. That's all we have open at the moment. But first, you have to figure out how to get in."

"Who do you think I am?" I ask him. My voice has lowered to a whisper even though there is no one else there around us.

"Colin Kelly, of course. Who else would you be?"

I squirm on the inside. I still don't know who this man is.

"Colin," he continues, "anything I can help you with, you let me know."

"How do I get inside?" I ask.

"I thought you'd never ask," he says. Then he stops his carving and shows me what he's been making. My eyes widen in surprise. It's a key. "Here you go," he says, "but I can't remember where the lock is. Somewhere around here." He stands up and dusts some of the snow off himself, and searches around the door, among all the carvings. I follow him, too, not sure what I should be searching for.

"Can't you find it?" he says.

As I examine the door more closely, I see familiar patterns, like those on the Mirror: sparrows on twigs, within the leaves and berries. Then, decorated within the carvings, I find a beautiful pheasant trying to fly over a seemingly insurmountable wall. I could have sworn that carving wasn't there before.

My fingers glide along the bird that cannot fly high enough, and I notice a fissure along the wings. Lightly, I push the seemingly movable feathers, and the whole set of wings opens, as though the bird could actually take flight. There, in its little feet, it holds a lock with a keyhole. I try the key, and it's a perfect fit.

"Aha," the Whittler says. "You found the way!"

I turn the key, and a large door opens. I can't help but wish Uncle Felix could be here to see all this.

"We don't just let anyone in at this hour, you know. Only those who are truly desperate."

Great.

I move forward in slow, cautious steps, across a mosaic stone floor, elegant and colorful. I'm tracking in substantial amounts of sludge behind me. Somehow, the Whittler hands me a clean pair of boots about my size. I think he pulled them off a shelf at the side of the entry.

"You cannot go walking around here all muddy." His fluffy hair seems to fluff up a little more. "Do you know how much work it takes to maintain this floor?"

"Thank you." Despite the awkwardness, I gratefully remove my shoes and put on the new ones, and then, he points me toward the last door at the end of a long central hallway.

"By the way," he says, "I'm working on a little project right now inside the Cathedral, and I sure could use some help. Through the Keeper grapevine, I heard you have the interest and the skill. Would you care to come join me?"

I'm surprised by his request, and as wonderful as it sounds, I need to contend with the Duke, not busy myself with whittling projects in the cathedral.

"Maybe another time," I say.

His eyes momentarily sadden with a downcast gaze, but then he brightens up again.

"Alright, if that's what you want," he says, and he leaves through a door that opens out of nowhere, along the hall he just directed me down, only a few steps to my left.

On my way along the hall, I notice the carvings in the entry, similar to the ones I'd seen on the front door. I push open the door to a space with about a dozen beds in it, half nestled into the walls, while the others stand in the middle. They are made of black-stained wood, engraved with the familiar patterns of leaves and branches.

A lady points me to a bunk in the middle.

I motion to a spot in a corner. "How about over there?"

I don't wait for her answer and walk to the bed I want to crash in. Thankfully, the lady doesn't protest, and I claim my bunk.

After I wash up, I position myself far into my nook up against the wall and under my cloak—no one should be able to see what I'm doing here—and unbundle the Mirror.

"Show me Molly," I whisper to the Mirror. "Did she cross the gate?"

I watch as Molly, hood down, mingles with the people of the caravan. She has smeared dirt on herself, especially over her birthmark.

"What's your purpose?" one of the guards asks.

"To visit family," she answers. That's no lie, since Molly wants to find her mother, but I wonder if her mother will be the sort of family she's hoping for.

"Last name?" the guard asks her.

"Kelly." Did she just use my last name? Why? I thought she would have hated me, and everything to do with me. My insides tighten.

Despite her choice, they allow her in. She's alright.

"Show me the Duke," I ask the Mirror.

The Duke and his Keepers are talking to Sir Jasper. I guess he made it in after the caravan, but now he is giving the Head Keeper a hard time.

"How could you not find them?" the Duke asks Sir Jasper. The Head Keeper doesn't answer. "Hopefully we won't have to suffer your incompetence much longer."

The Duke rides past him and the guards, and through the gate, into the city.

My blood is boiling. Sir Jasper didn't turn us in, but as Head Keeper, why isn't he doing more against the Duke? Doesn't he realize everything the Duke has done and that ultimately, the Duke wants to destroy him and take his place?

I ask the Mirror, "Why isn't Sir Jasper stopping the Duke?"

The Mirror ripples to an image of Sir Jasper speaking with the Ruler.

"The boy deserves his punishment. He betrayed not only the Duke, but by prematurely taking the Remedy and keeping information about the Mirror for himself, he is a traitor. He has no loyalty and cannot be trusted," the Ruler says.

"I believe he deserves another chance to do what's right," Sir Jasper says. "He's been misled by the Duke. The Duke is the one who needs to be disciplined."

"He's too important," the Ruler says. "Without him, the cities will not have access to the Remedy."

"There are other ways to travel and protect the people from the creatures," Sir Jasper responds.

"The Remedy is the easiest way, and you know it."

"Let me at least talk to him about where he obtains it from. Give me a chance to challenge him!"

The Ruler shakes her head, no. She's too scared of the Duke, and her fear is crippling the wellbeing of the cities. I realize now, Sir Jasper has his hands tied. However, if the Duke's control over the Remedy is the source of his power, then maybe I can help change that. If no one else can do something about the Duke, then maybe I can.

I lie there on the bed, thinking more about what to do, then pull myself up. I think about the people the Duke has harmed over the years, but the brief story Charlotte told us about Saint Raphael keeps coming back to me.

"What is the significance of Saint Raphael to the Duke?" I ask the Mirror.

One image flashes after another. He evacuated the city on the pretext that the creatures had breached the walls. My father had tried to stop him, but he had been too late. So many people died, except for those he selected and those the reindeer helped to safety.

No one thinks Saint Raphael is inhabited, *but it is*. It isn't a destroyed city. There are farmers there. That's where the Duke grows the plants and makes the Remedy. I can hardly believe it. How is this possible?

I sit up, pushing my hands through my hair, as though that could help me think more clearly about everything. How can no one else know about this?

I lie the Mirror down and think. How do I handle this information? I need to tell others. That's what I need to do. But who can I trust?

I set out to find a quiet room where I won't be disturbed. Eventually, I discover a study with a small desk. I light a candle and pull out parchment, ink, and a quill. There, I write down all the information I can garner about Saint Raphael and the Remedy production.

I wish the Mirror could tell the future, and that I could see how this will all play out and what the Duke's plans are, but unfortunately, all I can do is gather clues. The reality is, I already know. It takes me a while, but I eventually figure out the Duke wants control over all the cities. Not only does he want Sir Jasper's power, but the Ruler's, as well. I should have known that without even looking at the Mirror. It all makes sense now. But I might be the one person who can most effectively stand in his way.

I compose a letter to each of the Ruler and Sir Jasper, keeping them anonymous. I'm hoping to keep the Mirror a secret for as long as possible. And, while I don't trust the Ruler, I think I can count on her at least to want to preserve her own power.

I need to deliver the letters, but delivering them to the Ruler and Sir Jasper is not the simplest of tasks, even with the Mirror. I ask the Mirror what the easiest way for me to deliver the letter is, and it shows me the Whittler.

Who is that man? I will have to investigate him later, but for now, I trust the Mirror and go find him with my letters.

The fluffy man is in the cathedral, like he said he would be.

Around us are long, ornate wooden pews and tall, engraved wooden columns. At the heart of it all is an altar covered with embroidered fabric, as well as a thick garland of pines and berries. The Whittler is engraving something into the side of it.

"Excuse me?" I say.

"You've come to help me?" he asks, his eyebrows shooting up with joy.

"Actually, no. I have two letters here, and I was wondering if you could help me deliver them. They are incredibly important. And I don't have a wax or seal to close them."

He takes the papers I hand him, reading each of the addresses, his forehead creasing more and more.

"What is this about?" he asks.

I almost want to tell him everything. It would be nice to talk to someone about what the Duke did.

"Righting terrible wrongs. Can you help me?"

The man nods. He takes one of the candles from the church and lets wax dribble on to the fold of each envelope, then seals each one with his thumb print. "I will make sure they arrive safely."

I dig into my cloak for some coins, but the man refuses. Instead, he hands me a leather pouch.

"Accept this gift from me instead. I was so happy to see you, I couldn't help myself. And you look like you could use some cheering up."

"Thank you," I say, resigning myself to his kindness. I wonder what he has given me.

I return to the common room and to my bunk. I examine the little package, wondering at the same time if my letters will make any difference. The Duke's wrongs are so much greater than anything I could have imagined.

After lying down a while, I'm finally able to unfasten the leather pouch the Whittler gave me. Inside, I find a new set of lock picking tools with more beautiful carved wooden handles than I ever could have imagined, as well as a whittling tool with a small block of wood. There is a note that is attached:

You are an artist.

Do not neglect your gifts, and use them for good.

The Whittler

I look over each piece with care, then begin to fiddle with the piece of wood and carving tool. I'm not sure what I will carve, but this fresh start at something does cheer me up. I don't know how to use the Mirror to stop the Duke, but maybe I can rest a little for now.

CHAPTER 29
Molly

Wandering down a few streets, I'm not sure which way to go or where exactly I am. I want to see my mother, and I know she lives on Crumb Street, but I don't know where that is. I decide to ask a few passersby about my mom's address, but they pretend like they don't see or hear me. I guess I don't look very appealing.

I hear music in the distance, maybe some violins, and I decide to follow the sound. I have no other way of knowing where to go, since Colin has the Mirror now, and people won't talk to me. As the music becomes louder, I find myself in one of the city's open-air markets, where everything seems smothered in festive decorations and new products that have arrived from Saint Michael.

I walk by all the stands and their delicious food displays, realizing just how hungry I am. I can't help but stare at the pastries and baked goods that are in the stalls. Golden dough, baked apples, creams, honey, butter. It's all too delicious for me to handle, and the people who are enjoying them seem so happy. One woman is sharing a waffle with a young man. They are walking close to each other, affectionately arm in arm and happy. What I would give to be strolling through these aisles with a young man and a waffle, not a care in the world, content, and licking the sweetness off my fingers, with someone who is glad to be with me.

As I continue through the stands, my hand, almost as though acting as a separate entity from me, slips out from under my cloak toward some gorgeous baked goods. Not only am I tempted to steal something, but I almost carry it out. At the very last moment, the woman running the stand makes eye contact with me, and I hold back. But one moment later, and I would have stolen from her.

Just then, a guard comes down the aisle toward me. He must have seen my almost theft, too. I can't, under any circumstances, get into trouble with him.

"What are you doing here?" he asks.

"Enjoying this market," I say.

"You're a filthy mess. You don't belong here. Come back when you are clean," he barks at me. It's embarrassing as people stop and stare.

As I turn to leave, the woman who had been working in the stall—and who saw me almost steal—runs after me.

"Miss!" she shouts, and once she catches up with me, hands me a waffle smothered with sweet goodness. "I saw you admiring the food," she continues, "and I thought to myself, she doesn't mean harm. She just seems hungry. I hope you will enjoy it." She glances at my birthmark even though I try to keep it covered.

"Thank you," I say, accepting the delicious smelling waffle, somewhat in disbelief.

"You're welcome," she says. Her face is smiley and rosy.

"Do you happen to know where Crumb Street is?"

She smiles with a huge grin. "Of course! Just go straight, then take the third right. You are not too far away."

"Thanks, again," I say, and I take a bite of the waffle. It's even more wonderful than I had imagined.

I make my way to Crumb Street, eating my delicious waffle. Despite the late hour, many people stroll down the streets for evening walks. It would be wonderful to have friends and family to walk through these streets with, and as I continue along, I can't help but wonder where Colin is, and also, about what it will be like to see my mother.

Finally, I find my mother's dark plum colored door, and above it, the golden numbers, 250. My pulse quickens. *Should I really knock?*

I take a deep breath and knock on the door.

No one answers.

I persist with the knocker, but still no one answers. My heart sinks. If only my mother had been home. Now what?

At the last possible second, just as I'm about to leave and try to figure out my next move, someone opens. It's a man—tall and strongly built, with a narrow face, a well-trimmed mustache, and fine clothes. He taps his fingers on the door frame as his eyes glance over me.

"How may I help you?" he asks.

I hadn't thought about how to ask for my mother. Should I call her Mrs. Fitzpatrick? What last name does my mother go by now? I didn't think to ask the Mirror. And how am I supposed to introduce myself? I can't tell this stranger my real name.

"I'm here to see the woman of the house," I say.

The man's brow furrows.

"She's my mother. I'm her daughter."

"Your mother?"

"You don't know her name?" he continues.

"Anna," I say, hoping her first name will do. In fact, I'm not sure what my mother's last name is right now.

"If you truly are her daughter, show me your face," he says.

He waits, still tapping his fingers on the door frame.

When I lower my scarf and hood, he smiles.

"You look like her. I'm sorry I was rude when you first arrived and that it took me so long to come to the door," he says. "I hadn't fully grasped the situation. Unfortunately, she's not here right now."

After his initial inspection of me, his eyes seem to refuse to connect with mine.

"How did you find her?" he asks.

"I asked a lot of people," I say. I hadn't thought about how I would explain my presence. I obviously can't tell him about the Mirror.

"Never mind. You shouldn't be here," he says. "Your presence could put you both at risk."

"But I wanted to see her," I say. My heart is shattering like porcelain does when it hits a stone floor. "It's been so long."

The man gives me a fleeting warm look.

"I imagine you need a place to stay," he says. "We can't have you stay here. However, there is a nearby hotel that can accommodate you for a short while. We can cover your costs there several nights. You look like you could use some freshening up, and your mother can have breakfast with you in the morning. Please let us offer that."

Though I feel uneasy about the situation, I nod. After all, I have no idea who this man is, and I don't feel like I'm in a good position to ask him.

"Give the management this. They'll understand." He scribbles a name on a piece of paper with instructions on how to find the hotel and gives me a card. "She'll see you in the morning," he adds.

With that, the man closes the door. My heart is heavy, and I don't know what to think, but I would really like to have breakfast with my mother.

I find the hotel unexpectedly nice, with a big, wrought iron gateway, large windows, and a roundabout for carriages. Two young men stand outside waiting to help arriving patrons. As I approach, they eye me suspiciously.

"I was given instructions to come and meet someone here."

I pull out the card and note, trying to hand the information to one of them. He pushes them away and laughs.

I'm not sure what to do. I don't want to make a scene, but I don't want to walk away, either.

"Is everything all right?" a tiny woman from inside the front door asks.

I hold out the card and note. "I'm supposed to meet someone here," I say.

The woman's head tilts toward me with curiosity, then her brow furrows in concern. Finally, she motions for me to follow her.

"Walk with me," she says.

The young man who had first refused me opens the door for us and stands aside.

She welcomes me into the hotel, onto a deep wood floor. The interior is decorated with holly garlands, as well as candles, and the air smells like cinnamon. After the woman helps me check-in, we climb a grand staircase, and she personally takes me to my designated room. There, a thick carpet cushions my feet, and a large four poster bed layered with fluffy blankets and satin pillows sits in the middle of the floor. I don't think I've ever seen anything so marvelous in all my life.

"I'll have several dresses brought up to you, as well as a warm bath," the woman says.

"Why are you being so nice to me?" I ask.

"If I were in your shoes, I would want someone to be kind to me, and with the reference from the Ruler's own brother, how could we not help you?"

The Ruler's brother? What is my mother doing with him? Are they somehow connected to the Duke?

"What time is your meeting tomorrow morning? We can be sure to wake you up in time, if you would like."

"I was only told breakfast in the morning, but if you could wake me up, I would really appreciate it." As tired as I am, I'm also exceedingly anxious about meeting my mother and wonder how I will be able to sleep.

After the woman leaves, and someone brings up dresses and pours me a hot bath, I wash and prepare for bed. Despite everything, I don't even remember falling asleep.

CHAPTER 30
Colin

After I wake up, I realize I have slept several hours, but that it is still night. Thank goodness, because I need to check on the Duke.

"Where is the Duke?" I ask the Mirror.

The image in the Mirror ripples to him riding through the city.

"What has he been up to?" I ask.

The image ripples to a purple door: that's where Molly's mother lives. The Duke is speaking with a man. He tells him that if Molly were to visit, he should alert him. *How do I put a stop to this?*

"Where is Molly?" I need to warn her.

The Mirror shifts and shows me she is fast asleep in a hotel room bed.

"Where is the Duke staying?"

I wonder if it's the same hotel as Molly, but the Mirror ripples to the Hall of Prayers. He's staying *here*. I should have guessed that since this is where my father always stayed when he came to this city. The Duke should be back soon, but not just yet. I'm going to end his plans once and for all, and this time, Molly isn't here to interfere—and she'll be the first one to thank me for it. I'm going to save her, after all.

I push down a lever and open a concealed door to a long, shrunken corridor. It leads to a spiral staircase, as the Mirror predicted, and I ascend the steps, two by two until I reach the third floor and slide into the hallway, shutting the secret passage door behind me. It's a nice hallway, with a thick carpet and wood joists along the ceiling. I count to the fifth door on the left. Before I work on the door, two people walk through—likely pilgrims here for prayer.

Using my new lock picking set, I break into the Duke's room. Despite the obscurity, I take a quick inventory of his belongings. The notebook is there, on his desk, its pages spread out everywhere. Being alone here is eerie, especially after I latch the door behind me.

I position myself behind a big chair and tighten my grip around the handle of my knife. If all goes as planned, the Duke should enter anytime now, and I will be ready to throw my blade at him, ending his abuses, once and for all.

Soon enough, keys jingle outside the door. My hands are trembling. Will I even be able to throw the blade properly? I position myself to attack, but at the last second I glance around the room for a place to hide—the armoire.

By the time the bedroom door opens, I have barely slid in and shut myself in. I hope the Duke won't need anything from my concealed nook, and that he hasn't heard the creaking of the hinges. My heart is beating so loud inside of me, it hurts my ears.

Through a sliver of an opening, I watch as my former mentor throws his belongings on the bed. After pulling off his outer clothing and shirt, he sits at his desk, in front of the Fitzpatricks' notebook, and lights a few candles. He pours himself a drink and studies. I wonder how long this will go on before he goes to sleep.

I've never felt claustrophobic before, but the walls of this armoire seem to be leaning in toward me. I am cramped, and my foot muscles are full of pins and needles. Even if I could leave, I probably wouldn't be able to stand up. And when I shift, the wood creaks, so I can't even adjust myself.

The Duke has been reading forever. Can't he be finished already?

After what feels like hours, the Duke finally blows out the diminished candles and moves on to his bed. I wait for his breathing to steady and deepen. He's asleep. This is the opportunity I had been hoping for. If I don't make my move, he will go after Molly. I have to stop the Duke now.

As I push the armoire door open and crawl out of the bottom of my hole, I try to control the unraveling of my mind. My heart is relentlessly pounding. Everything is creaking, but the Duke is in a deep sleep.

My knife is in my hands. It will be easy to slice his throat, just like what he did to that woman in the wilderness. This is exactly what he trained me to do: to not care and do what needs to be done. As I approach the bed, sweat makes my hand and fingers slippery and my sense of vision murky. I'm standing over the Duke. His face is frightening even while he sleeps. Why am I scared? I have the power here, and I am using it for good—to rid the cities of this ruthless, manipulative leader. Our whole society will be much better off after I do this.

Suddenly, there is a knocking at the door.

The Duke shifts on his bed.

I've taken too long, and I scramble to retreat back into the armoire.

I'm not fully in when the Duke shouts, "What is it?" He sits up.

"She's taken the bait," the person behind the door says loudly.

The Duke pulls himself out of the bed. I barely tuck my feet into the enclosed space.

"I'll be right out," he says, and he lights a candle again.

The Duke throws on the shirt that he arrived in and opens the door. In the frame are two guards, with whom he rushes away.

Once stillness falls on the room, I crawl my way out of the bottom of the armoire again. I go to the door, but I can't open it yet. I push my head and hands against it. I'm a fool and clobbered with defeat. Molly isn't safe. I want to scream, but can't. I want to kick the door in, but can't. I want to do something, anything, but can't. I have the most powerful tool in all the cities and can accomplish nothing with it.

CHAPTER 31
Molly

Someone is knocking at my bedroom door.

"Breakfast," a woman's voice calls from the other side.

I wake up and put on one of the dresses I've been given—it's a cotton green one—fix my hair, and rush downstairs.

"We have a private room for you," a new woman says, and after we've gone down to the lobby, she motions me toward two wooden doors. She accompanies me inside and invites me to sit at a beautiful table. It is adorned with real silverware, a winter bouquet of flowers, and linen cloth and napkins.

I wonder how long it will be before my mother arrives. What will we talk about? It would be nice if I found out she had been longing for Hugo and me all these years.

A server arrives and tells me food is available. He lists a number of dishes, but all I can focus on is that he seems shaky when he speaks to me, as though he is very nervous to interact with me. After he disappears behind the swinging doors, my private room feels oddly still and empty, as though it is holding its breath.

Just as I'm about to stand up to investigate, the doors open again. The Duke's Keepers enter—the same ones whose lives I saved in the forest. My stomach drops.

I try to bolt, but my whole body is immovable, heavy like lead. And just like that, the Keepers surround me.

"Do you remember what the penalty for treason is?" a Keeper I saw before says, his eyes glimmering. "Because that's what happened to your father."

I launch everything I can put my hands on toward the assailing Keepers—knives, forks, and the vase on the table.

"You're outnumbered," the guard says, "and there are more guards outside as well. You may as well come nicely."

Just then, I manage to grab a chair and slam it into the nearest Keeper. He wasn't expecting the blow and is disoriented. I run to the exit, but as I push through, several hands pull me down and a hood is thrown over my head.

"Tie her up," someone orders.

They fasten my wrists and prod me forward with what feels sharp like the tips of spears. As my next steps envelop me into sudden cold, I know we've crossed the hotel's threshold and gone into the street. They push me into a rough wooden cart, then tie my feet.

"Where are you taking me?" I ask.

In response, I receive a massive hit over the head, and everything falls to nothingness.

CHAPTER 32
Colin

When I finally enter back into the hallway, the world is spinning. Instead of moving, I stop and my back slides down against the wall. I fold into myself, on the floor, head between my knees. I have failed my family, as well as Molly. Everybody.

It's hard to know how long I'm there for, except that after some time, the sound of approaching voices finally snaps my thoughts into focus. I stand up as two of the Duke's Keepers appear from the end of the hall. When they see me, their eyes widen and they hurry toward me. It's time to run. The hallway is relatively long, but they are blocking the exit I had planned on using.

I rush in the opposite direction, hoping there is another way out. Unfortunately, it leads to a dead end. My pursuers come after me like angry dogs, shouting words that may as well be barking.

"You have nowhere to run, Colin Kelly," I hear one say.

Nothing like stating the obvious.

"Were you trying to enter the Duke's chambers?" he asks. "Further disgracing your family's name?"

We lock eyes. "The Duke stole something from me." Too bad everything he stole, I can never get back.

"Why share your grievances with us when you can share them with the Duke directly?" he says.

Can I push through them and make a run for it? I have to.

As I attempt to rush past them, the first shoves me and the second takes a punch. The latter misses me, and I push him into his friend. Next thing I know, I'm flying down the hall. When I open the concealed door, another Keeper appears there, ascending the stairs toward me. When he sees me running at him, he pulls out two knives and points them at me. I have no way forward, unless I want to lose a limb, and with the other Keepers behind me, I'm three to one. This is a terrible situation.

The Keeper with the knives lunges at me, and a blade almost slices through my left shoulder. Without thinking, I reach up to take hold of his wrists with both hands, twisting.

"Do you not know who I am?" I shout.

Unexpectedly, the Keeper with the knives freezes, and I grab one of the blades—from the sharp side. My hand is bleeding profusely. Still, I manage to pivot the knife on to him. The Keeper drives forward with his other blade, knocking his lost one out from my hand. The two other Keepers close in as well. As much as I try to fight them, there is no winning for me here. All I can do is try not to act cowardly, fighting as best I can. They have their hands on me and their blades on me, and I am overtaken. The Keepers take me down and tie my hands up. We walk many passageways heading downward. The whole time, all I can think about is how they treated me over the notebook, and how much worse it will be if the Duke finds out about the Mirror.

We reach an area completely different, where everything is stone and dark and damp. Somehow, I sincerely doubt we're still anywhere near the Hall of Prayers. It smells like excrement down here, for one. And for two, these halls aren't lined with rooms, but with cells.

A few torches light our way, but barely. They take me around a large quadrangle. I glance at the locks as we go by. I've never tried a prison door lock. Wasn't this Molly's original request from me, to try to break Hugo out of a prison cell?

"Help," one of the prisoners shouts from down the hall. The shout echoes through the whole place. He's pounding at his door. "Get me out of here!" he screams at the top of his lungs. "Save me," the prisoner cries out. "Please, save me."

I wish I could do something. I wish I knew what that was all about.

We go down one more hall, and the Keepers shove me into my own cell. Pitch black. Damp ground. Freezing.

As I sit, many thoughts begin to plague me, but one in particular: how will I be able to keep the Mirror from the Duke?

CHAPTER 33
Molly

I drift in and out of consciousness, but I know I'm lying on a stone floor. Hours must have passed by—maybe more. I can't tell because everything is darkness, and I'm very hungry and thirsty. Besides the filth and rats scurrying along the walls, only cold fills the cell with me.

Then, I hear footsteps.

"Are you hungry?" The voice sends shivers down my spine.

The door opens, and the Duke enters with several of his Keepers. He will want information from me: about the notebook, Colin, and maybe even the Mirror. I am scared to be alone here with them. I have no way to protect myself, and no fight left in me.

One of the Keepers hands me a bowl of soup and some bread.

"Your last meal," the Duke says, "if you don't cooperate."

The warm liquid is soothing going down, even though I cannot clearly identify its contents.

The Duke pulls my father's notebook out, the maps that led to the Mirror wanting to fall free from the surrounding pages. Then, he takes one of the Keepers' torches and sets the notebook on fire.

"You and Colin already have the Mirror, don't you? This book is useless now, isn't it?" By the light of the flames, the Duke's features are immaculate and terrifying at the same time. His eyes reflect the blaze of the fire, like they want to burn me up. "When you went to find your mother," he continues, "you confirmed you used the Mirror. There was no other way you could have known where she was."

Meanwhile, flames consume my father's notebook. At least he had managed to keep the Mirror from the Duke.

"Where is the Mirror? If you help me," he says, "you will be rewarded with more than you can possibly imagine. You will become a princess and a Keeper among Keepers. And everyone in the cities will remember you as the hero who helped restore our cities."

I sigh deeply. The Duke's face suddenly appears kind, like he would move mountains and conquer the world for me. Part of me is even momentarily drawn to him. How can one person have so much charisma? His words are like honey to my soul, because everything he says is exactly my dream. The truth is, I have no idea where it is. And the other truth is, every word that man speaks is poison.

"I don't know where the Mirror is," I say.

When I don't answer favorably, his face transforms from perfect goodness to that of a man consumed with greed. The Duke's voice explodes out of him, expecting obedience. "Where is the Mirror? Answer me now, or you'll be heading for the cliffs."

When I shake my head no, he whacks the bowl of soup in my face.

I try to wipe the liquid away, while simultaneously readying myself for the next blow.

"Get rid of her," he says as he leaves. "Over the cliffs—tonight. I'm almost certain Colin has the Mirror now."

So that's it? This is the end of my story? The Duke will be going after Colin now, but at least he has the Mirror to protect himself.

Just as he walks out the cell door, the Duke pauses and faces me once more. He is framed by the cell door with the Keepers at his side.

"You know, no one will miss you. No one will even realize you're gone. If anything, I'm doing you a favor."

When they go, they lock the door behind themselves, and everything goes dark again. I am alone with the rats, but they at least are better than the Duke. I wonder how much time I have left.

CHAPTER 34
Colin

Footsteps echo over the cold stone corridor outside my cell. As they resonate around me, tension cripples my breathing. If it's the Duke, how will I keep the Mirror's location a secret? I don't know if I can stand up to him.

A key turns in the lock to my door, and the rusty hinges grind open. A man enters, and two people follow, bearing torches—presumably Keepers. At first, I think it's the Duke, but when the man crouches in front of me, I realize my mind played a trick on me. It's Sir Jasper, not the Duke.

He approaches me gently. "I'm here for you, Colin."

I take in the deep lines of his face and his gray hair. Normally it's pulled back in a tidy bun, but tonight his hair is wild. He's also wearing his ornate glasses, their gold and gems glistening in the torchlight. I don't like him seeing me in this condition, sitting on these prison stones and in the muck. I can't help but wonder if he's after the Mirror, just like the Duke.

"The Whittler told me you were here," he says. "I can lead you out, if you want."

"What's in it for you?" I ask.

"I'm a Keeper. Not all Keepers act like this, but this is what I do. I'm here for you," he says. Sir Jasper takes my face in his hands in a fatherly sort of way and examines me through his crazy spectacles, close enough that his big nose almost touches my face.

I shift awkwardly. "Aren't you here for the Mirror?"

"I'm actually here for Molly, as well as for you," he says.

"Is Molly here?"

"Not anymore. I didn't find out about her until it was too late. She needs both our help, Colin—more than you can know. The Duke's guards are already taking her to the cliffs." The Head Keeper sits on the floor next to me. "Come with me now, or stay and wait for the Duke and a life hooked on Remedy. In fact, he should arrive here any minute now. But it will cost you Molly's life."

"Why did you rescue me the other day, outside the walls?"

His eyes lock onto mine. "Did you know what the Duke's objective was for you that day?"

I shake my head no.

"I'm almost certain he wanted to be rid of you and your family once and for all. Before that, he had only ever hoped you might lead him to the Mirror, and he must have deemed you no longer useful and let you fall prey to your own desires. But you should ask the Mirror."

"But he gave me Remedy," I say.

"Only what was sufficient to give you the illusion of safety."

So Sir Jasper was looking out for me.

"Are you ready to come help me?"

"The reality is, my past decisions foretell a probability of future failure rather than success."

"That's not how probability works. You might still be able to help her." He pats me on the back and motions me toward the exit. "But we need to hurry."

I stand, and immediately, we leave the cell, two Keepers in tow, and we hurry into a neighboring corridor.

Not moments later, the Duke's voice calls out for me. Though I can't see my own face, I'm pretty sure all the blood has drained out of it.

The Keepers extinguish their torches. We scurry into a nearby cell, and Sir Jasper silently shuts its door behind us.

The Duke calls for me, again, anger in his voice now. The sound is nerve-racking. Sir Jasper takes me by the shoulders, and I start to breathe again—I hadn't realized that I had stopped.

"Find him!" the Duke shouts, and then footsteps scatter.

Are they able to track us? I hope I don't do something dumb to give us away.

Someone is coming. I hold my breath again. Is it the Duke out there, or a Keeper?

After the sound of the footsteps diminishes, Sir Jasper opens the door back up.

"Follow me," he says.

Before I know it, we are hurrying down yet another hallway and find our way to a hidden spiral staircase. Sir Jasper grips the stairway railing and motions the Keepers and me forward.

It's not much different from the one I had originally found, except this one is more rickety, quite a bit older, and, judging by the cobwebs and dust, infrequently used.

We travel further, along several long corridors, until we arrive at a small wooden door.

Where are we going?

After he dismisses the two Keepers, Sir Jasper pulls a ring of keys from his pocket and shoves me into what appears to be a vast hollow space. I cannot see anything, but smell a strong, sweet fragrance all around me—is it incense?

He guides me through the obscurity, except ahead, one lone, mesmerizing light flickers, but its light stretches far. Sir Jasper hands me a candle and takes one for himself. We carry our wicks to the lonesome flame and light them, and everything around us becomes illuminated with glimmering gold.

"Is this the Cathedral of Saint Selaphiel?" I ask.

He nods. "Selaphiel is the angel of prayers—an example of the power of prayer in battle. We will need to pray now if we are to succeed."

He brings me into one of the pews and kneels down, motioning for me to join him.

"Why?" I ask.

Sir Jasper peers over his golden glasses at me. "As you admitted yourself, you don't have the strength or capacity to help Molly—and neither do I. So now, we will seek strength in humility, from beyond ourselves."

I run a nervous hand through my hair.

"And ask for strength for Molly, too," he adds. "She will need it more than us."

I bow my head and close my eyes, pressing my forehead against the wood of the pew. It smells of fresh wood polish. I don't know how to pray, but the image of the ribbon that kept Molly and me together in the river appears in my mind, and I ask God for new sort of ribbon, that would help both of us survive this.

After a little while, Sir Jasper taps me on the shoulder.

When I open my eyes, the Head Keeper sits up in the pew, folding his hands in front of himself.

"Per Keeper requirements, I assume you know how to swim," he says.

"Yes," I answer.

"Good. Since the Duke is about to throw Molly over the cliffs, it seems like you will begin this new part of your journey in water. Specifically, sea water."

"What?"

"The only way to save Molly is after the Duke throws her in. That way, he will believe she has died and won't continue pursuing her."

I can't believe what I'm hearing, but Sir Jasper has a genuinely serious expression on his face. He means every word he says.

My jaw tightens. The crazy thing is, I would jump off the cliffs for Molly, but this can't work. His plan is doomed to failure. I'm not strong enough for this.

"We'll get caught, or I'll fail, and then, she will drown," I say. "Besides, can't she die from the fall alone?"

"We have no other choice," he replies. "We have to at least try."

I lean my head against the pew in front of us and sigh. How can we wait until after she falls?

Meanwhile, Sir Jasper pulls a bundle from his pocket and hands it to me.

"What's this?" I ask.

"Open it up."

I unwrap the fabric to find lock picking tools from the Whittler.

"You might still need them," he says. "You left them in the Duke's room, along with a very sharp knife."

There is only one way forward for me now.

I want to help Molly, but I have no idea how Sir Jasper expects me to do this. The crunching of wheels and horse's hooves on the cobblestones grate on my thinking. I wish I could have silence to consider through what I need to do.

We continue to ride in the carriage until we are out of the inner walls of the city, and then we race through the farmlands leading to the sea and to some fishing communities.

"You know," I start, "I care about her, but it's still strange. Her father might not have killed my parents, but he certainly didn't help protect them. Not to mention, the family kept the Mirror for themselves after that. They could have helped make things right, but they didn't. And then, she hid the Mirror from me. I understand why, but I don't think I can ever fully trust her." I don't know why I'm telling Sir Jasper all this, but I need to talk to someone about it.

"What do you think your father or your Uncle Felix would have advised you?"

"My guess is that they would have focused on the good rather than the bad. Both of them always saw the best in people. And I *do* care about her. What we've survived through, I could never forget."

Sir Jasper nods. "I'm glad to hear you say that. It says a lot about you."

As we approach the coast, the land is more jagged, the road is bumpier, and the smell of salt rides on the air.

"I will drop you off here," Sir Jasper says.

"Over here? Isn't this a bit far?"

"The Duke might be hoping you will come, so under no circumstances can you let him see you. I will go on ahead to challenge him and his Keepers in order to distract them. The rest is up to you."

"This feels impossible," I say.

"It will be extremely difficult, but you have prayed, so now just take it one step at a time."

After sharing his unhelpful words, Sir Jasper lets me out of the carriage and then rides off toward the Duke and the gathering of guards around Molly. I hide among the tall, prickly grass lining the cliffs and sneak closer. From my spot, I watch as Sir Jasper approaches the cluster of the Duke and his Keepers. The Duke loudly reads charges about how Molly is a traitor and how deserving she is of her execution. Meanwhile, a cloth covers Molly's head, and chains constrain her hands and legs.

I peer over the edge of the cliff at the ocean below. They are very high, and the waves, beating on the rocky shore, are rough and relentless. Fear tries to paralyze my heart, but if I have to choose between fear and Molly, Molly wins. I can't let Molly die without being there for her.

I kneel. "God, please give me strength and ability to rescue Molly. Help me bring her to safety."

When I stand, a cloudless night sky stretches over the cliffs that loom ahead. I still have no idea what to do except move forward and scramble along the cliffside, hurtling myself through the brush, sprinting over rocks, pushing myself toward Molly. The cold night air burns through my lungs, and as the wind pushes against me, it's hard to stay focused.

I spot a slight protrusion in the cliff and climb down to it, to be closer to the water. I take off my boots and prepare myself to jump in after her. The dizzying height is terrifying, but I can't overthink it, or I won't do it. I only have so much time. I hope that in the darkness and with Sir Jasper distracting them, no one sees me.

CHAPTER 35
Molly

Heavy chains, throbbing muscles, cold and salty air. My head, still covered. Wood creaks under my bare feet. The sound and smell of the sea. Weights, designed to sink me to the ocean floor. Memories of my father. This is how he must have felt.

"Did you hear the news?" Even in my stupor, I recognize the Duke's voice. He's speaking low so only I can hear.

"Colin came to visit me, and he has decided to join me after all. He's agreed to hand over the Mirror and is ready to begin his new and prosperous life."

"After you murdered his family, I doubt that," I reply.

But part of me wonders. *Would* Colin give in to the Duke?

"You, on the other hand, have reached your final destination," he continues.

He yanks my hood off, and my eyes adjust. The Duke and some of his Keepers surround me, but also the immense, star-filled night sky. Despite my situation, I still have the power to choose what to focus on, and I will choose the beautiful.

"Look at me," he commands.

When I don't, he hits me across the face. My cheek stings, but I don't look at him. He grabs my face and forces me to. His disdainful eyes stare at me.

"You are a worthless girl. How you even made it to the selection is beyond me," he says, prodding me with the tip of a fighting spear.

"If I'm so worthless, why are you going through all this trouble over me?"

CHAPTER 36
Colin

All at once, the Keepers are silent, and there, against the night sky, Molly falls helplessly.

I rush to a protruding lip of rock beneath me, my muscles moving with all the coordination and strength I can muster.

Molly hits the water.

I ease a step back, then propel myself forward, as far from the edge of the rocks as possible. As I jump, the wind currents sweep at me, but I try my best to make my body as tight as an arrow and then prepare myself for the shock of the water.

When I pierce through the surface of the water, the freezing sea engulfs me. It is so cold it burns and leaves me disoriented. I have to pull my thoughts together before Molly drowns.

I kick myself to the surface, take a deep breath, and then dive back under the water. I keep my eyes open, but they might as well not be because everything is obscured by the darkness. I still myself and listen: water moves everywhere. I swim down and grab onto a rock on the ocean floor to avoid drifting to the surface. This is when I need the miracle to happen. After thinking a moment, I push and swim toward where I think she should be. That's the best I can do.

First, I find the chains. Then, her hair and her face.

I hardly have any air left, and she most likely has none. I must bring her to the surface.

The weight of the chains prevents me from easily moving her, but as best I can, I take hold of her, and, with all my might, heave her toward the shore. The current pulls me forward, the roll of the waves guiding me. The water both suffocates me and helps me carry her. I have to make it to the surface.

Finally, I hoist Molly's head out of the water, and I hope she can take a gulp of air. Then, I kick myself up above the waves, just enough to catch a breath.

I breathe. I'm not deprived of air anymore. But a wave is coming, and it would have been difficult enough for me to scramble over the rugged rocks on my own. How do I keep us both safe? I grab on to the edges of the rocks with one hand. A wave lifts us. I tuck Molly's head against me—the pounding surf could easily crush her skull against the rocks. The wave thrusts us forward and slams us down. We hit the jagged protrusions hard. My shoulder and hip take the brunt of the impact, and then, the wave recedes. I work to pull Molly forward. Another wave pummels us, but it's not nearly as strong.

I gather my strength and succeed at hoisting Molly onto the shore. There, she lies in a tangled mess of chains and seaweed. I pull her to further safety, in a nook within the cliffside, and check that she is breathing. Although she must be hurting in a hundred places, I can feel her pulse, and she is breathing.

"I missed you," Molly says in a barely audible voice.

I wrap my arms around her and pull her into a hug, warming her. Her body is shaking uncontrollably.

"I missed you, too," I say and can't help but kiss the top of her head.

I need to figure out how to bring her to safety. On one side, the cliff face towers over us, and on the other, the sea pounds at us. And I wonder, are any of the Duke's Keepers still above? I don't see anyone. It seems this nook is deep enough.

"I need to let go of you while I work on these locks," I say.

She nods.

I assess the irons that restrain her, then blow warm air over my hands, rubbing them together to restore my capacity for fine motor work. Finally, I pull out the Whittler's little set of lock picking tools from my pocket.

First, I work on the lock restraining her arms. My hand hurts from the slice it received when I was caught, and my fingers are clumsy, but I work steadily. When the bolt clicks open, I unravel the chains from her upper body.

Just then, a whistle pierces the air from above, and a rope drops down.

"Sir Jasper," I say.

I take my tools and help Molly unfasten the chains holding her feet, then toss the chains and locks into the ocean. I smile as they fall into the waves.

After that, I help her stand up and secure the rope tightly around her.

"Will you be able to hang on?"

She nods yes, and before long, Sir Jasper is hoisting her up the side of the cliff. I'm not sure how he's doing it, but I'll ask questions later.

Once she is up, the Head Keeper drops the rope down again and hoists me up next. And when I make it up top, the Head Keeper tightly squeezes my shoulders.

"I'm so proud of you," he says, then wraps me in a blanket. He guides me through the brush to his carriage. Molly is already in there, all bundled up.

"Inside, there are dry clothes," he says.

Molly's already changed into some sort of long tunic. I climb in beside her, while Sir Jasper pulls out several more thick covers for us. He's like a father tucking in his children.

"You came for me," Molly says.

Sir Jasper smiles at me, wrinkling up his face.

"But where will we go?" she asks. "Won't the Duke find us?"

"Somewhere safe," Sir Jasper says. "And I'm going to the Ruler tonight, right after I settle you both in."

"I know this is risky, but I need to get the Mirror from the Hall," I say. Hopefully, it is still safe, and I can help keep track of the Duke with it.

"We can stop by quickly," Sir Jasper says.

After reattaching one of the horses to the carriage—I guess that's how he pulled us up—Sir Jasper drives us away.

Molly's eyes close as she leans her head against me.

"What are we going to do now?" she asks.

"I think we should give ourselves a little time to recover, then figure out how to help Sir Jasper and the Ruler hold the Duke accountable."

Molly smiles. "I'm glad we have Sir Jasper."

It comforts me too that we are not in this on our own.

We make an uneventful stop at the Hall, then arrive at a simple but elegant home. The facade is narrow, with noticeable stonework. Sir Jasper comes around to the carriage door.

"We must enter quickly. Cover your heads carefully."

Molly and I each use a blanket to conceal ourselves and hurry inside. Sir Jasper invites us in and lights some candles. The main room is warm with a low fire in the fireplace. Sir Jasper and I take Molly to a bedroom. I carry her while Sir Jasper shows me the way. Once she is tucked in, Sir Jasper sits with me by the fire in the main room.

"You know you are in grave danger," he says.

I nod. "As long as the Duke knows you have the Mirror, he will be doing everything he can to come after it."

"Could I just get some sleep for now?" I ask.

Sir Jasper pats me on the back. "We have a big day tomorrow," he says. "And you are right. You do need your rest, and I need to go talk with the Ruler now. I will show you to your room. We must talk more in the morning."

CHAPTER 37
Molly

A little bit chilly, I burrow deeper into a gray wool blanket and gaze out the nearby window. My body is aching, especially the throbbing pain around my sides—maybe some broken ribs? I'm not sure how long I have been asleep for, and it takes me a few moments to orient myself. Outside my window is a small courtyard-garden, in the middle of which stands a barren tree. Its dark bark is striking against the crisp snow around it. I bet during the other seasons, this is a full, lush garden.

Robed in deep indigo, Colin hurries across towards me, his footsteps crunching on the frosted gravel outside. When he sees me through the windowpane, he waves and comes close. My blood churns with joy at seeing him. It is strange to me that, besides Sir Jasper, he is the only person who knows I'm alive. Through the glass, he makes several cheerful, funny faces, and I can't help but laugh. I didn't know Colin had a funny side.

He motions that he is going to come around and talk to me. I fold my blankets and go to the mirror, sitting atop the marble fireplace, to check what I look like. My face is bruised and cut, and quite frankly, the injuries make my birthmark look like nothing. I've never looked worse, but what is there to do about it? I fix my hair, as best I can, and cover my shoulders with a thick shawl I find folded on the mantel.

Soon enough, there is a knock at my door. "It's me," Colin says.

When I open, he has a huge smile, but what catches my attention are the dark rings under his eyes. He's been through one terrible situation after another ever since we left Saint Michael—not just physically. At least, despite everything, his countenance is joyful.

"These are for you." He pulls a bouquet of winter greens and berries from behind his back and hands them to me.

"Thank you," I say, brushing my fingers over the different sprigs of the bouquet. I especially like the thistles. They are beautiful but prickly. "How did you find these?"

"I picked them from the backyard this morning while I was waiting for you to wake up and Sir Jasper to return. How are you doing?" He pushes a nervous hand through his hair.

"A little bit sore," I say. "But very thankful for you and Sir Jasper."

"I'm so sorry I left you at the city gates, Molly. I thought you were in my way, but the truth is, I can't handle any of this without you. I'm really sorry I did that. I hope you can forgive me."

His words mean a lot. I really missed him.

"Of course. It worked out for the good. See? I'm still here." I try to sound cheerful.

Colin is leaning up against the door frame now, a solemn look on his face. "This is going to sound strange, coming from me," he says, "but my parents used to say to love people, no matter what—that that's what it truly means to be a Keeper. I had forgotten about that, but there are many things I'm starting to remember better, now."

"That's amazing." I can see the difference in his demeanor. Something has definitely changed.

I shake my head, searching for the right words to say.

"I'm sorry about what happened with your trying to see your mom," he continues.

I shrug.

"If you want, we could investigate the whole situation in the Mirror."

Part of me thinks that would be great, but I'm also scared to find out what really happened. "Maybe I can talk with Sir Jasper about her," I say. I never really asked him about her, and now that I think about it, of all people, he would likely be able to provide the most insight. He always told Hugo and I that our parents loved us.

"Speaking of which, before he left to meet with the Ruler last night, he said he wanted to meet with me first thing this morning, but I can't find him. I don't know if he ever came back."

"Why don't you ask the Mirror?" I say.

"What if he's just taking a really long bath or slept in or something?"

Colin seems really worried.

"We should check," I insist.

"You're right." His eyes light up, and he straightens. "Follow me," he says. "I have something I want to show you, besides us checking up on him in the Mirror."

After I set down the bouquet, Colin guides me through a mural-covered hall, at the end of which is a wildly painted door, slightly ajar. He knocks on it softly, maybe just out of principle. When no one answers, we enter.

"I discovered this place by accident this morning when I was looking for Sir Jasper."

The room smells like melted wax and burning candles, and hundreds of strange trinkets glimmer along the walls. Two fancy matching sofas with lilies embroidered on them take up most of the space at the center of the room, as well as a tall grass-green cushioned chair by the desk.

"I somehow remember this place from a long time ago," I tell Colin, as I run my hands over the chair's thick fabric.

"I had a feeling you would like it in here. I think it might be a study he uses."

Colin offers me a biscuit from a tray on the desk. "I'm sure he would have offered you one," he says.

"Thank you." I decide to nibble on one of Sir Jasper's treats, mostly because I am really hungry.

"Do you know Sir Jasper is actually the oldest Keeper?" I say.

"He was a mentor to my father, actually," Colin answers, looking down at his hands. "Do you want some tea to go with those biscuits?" he asks, shifting his weight from one foot to the other.

He is doing everything he possibly can to be kind.

"I would love some."

Colin proceeds to look at the kettle and all the herbs for tea, but seems puzzled. "I've never actually made tea before," he admits.

I laugh and proceed to show him. We boil water on Sir Jasper's little stove and pour ourselves a cup each over dried mint leaves, with a bit of honey added.

We sit down across from each other. I can't help but choose the green chair. He leans back on his little sofa, and from behind his cup, peers at me curiously.

Drinking tea with him like this, is unexpectedly wonderful, like when all we had was each other.

He pulls the Mirror out.

"I guess we'd better check on our Head Keeper," he says. "Where is Sir Jasper?" he asks the Mirror.

The image in the Mirror ripples, and Sir Jasper appears—but he is tied up, with a hood over his head. When the image moves out, sand and rocks are by his feet, and he's in some sort of sea cave. In addition, a paper is attached to the front of him. It reads: *Bring me the Mirror before the tide rises, or this traitor drowns.* Then, the image fades.

Colin puts the Mirror down and closes his eyes. "It's the Duke's handwriting," he says grimly.

How can this be?

I pick up the Mirror. My hand is shaking. "How did the Duke capture Sir Jasper?"

The image ripples again, and the Ruler appears before us with Sir Jasper. They are in her formal throne room. While Sir Jasper tries to talk some sense into her about stopping the Duke, she hands a message to one of the guards. He in turn takes the missive to the Duke, in the next room over.

"So the Ruler is working with the Duke?" I ask the Mirror.

An icky, icy sensation comes over me as a series of images of the Duke and the Ruler unfold before me. I set the Mirror down.

Colin and I exchange frowns.

"I can't believe this," I say, and nervously rub dried mint leaves between my fingers. Their smell is calming.

"I'm not surprised," Colin says. "But I hadn't expected her to completely betray her duties to our cities." Bitterness saturates his voice.

"I think the Mirror just does that to people," I say. "She probably thinks that if she helps the Duke, she'll eventually get it."

"I'm surprised he even told her about it," Colin says. He stands up, pacing. "The Duke will do everything he can to get the Mirror, and has her eating from the palm of his hand. The cities are practically his. Sir Jasper couldn't have suspected the Ruler, but he doesn't know the Duke's power of manipulation the way I do."

"We have to do something. We must help Sir Jasper and stop him. We have the Mirror, and we make a pretty good team."

CHAPTER 38
Colin

Molly pinches her lips. "Do you have any ideas?"

"Even if we leave now, how could we possibly help him? We cannot give the Duke the Mirror, and we can't let the Duke see you," I say.

Molly has a big wool blanket wrapped around her shoulders. She wraps it around herself more tightly.

"You somehow managed to help me," she says.

I pace the room again. I need to focus. It's not just Sir Jasper I have to help, but I need to bring the Duke's malevolence to an end.

I pull out the Mirror. "How do I stop the Duke?" I ask it. I don't know if it can answer that question, but you never know.

The Mirror doesn't show me anything. I guess that's not the sort of question it can answer.

"The tide is going to rise," Molly's voice quivers. "We only have so much time."

"Show me Sir Jasper," I tell the Mirror.

Molly's holding her breath.

As the image shifts, a huddled-up, immobile shadow lying on sand and rocks appears in front of us. Like a gentle wind blowing over a pool of water, a closer image of the Head Keeper drifts over the Mirror and shows swelling and bruising covering his exposed skin.

"You figured out how to find the Mirror. Surely you can help solve this," I say.

"That was different. How did you help me?"

"Sir Jasper told me to pray and jump in the water after you."

"To pray? Maybe we should do that now?"

I'm slightly irritated at the suggestions, but we bow our heads. Then, for whatever reason, I actually go down on my knees.

"God," I say, "you know Molly and I have always wanted to be Keepers. Please help us rescue Sir Jasper and protect us and the Mirror against the Duke. We cannot do this on our own. We need your help."

After that, I sink into the nearest chair.

"I don't know," Molly says. "Maybe we could distract the Duke and the guards and then we could run in and get Sir Jasper?"

"Maybe we should kidnap the Ruler, and broker an exchange," I say sarcastically.

Molly ignores me. "What are all the ways to access the place where Sir Jasper is?" she asks the Mirror.

The image in the Mirror ripples again and shows us the entrance to a cave. It's well guarded. This is where the Duke and his Keepers are expecting to meet us.

"There has to be a better way," she continues.

"Are there other ways into the cave?" I ask the Mirror.

The image ripples again, and a crevice in the rocks appears.

I hadn't expected the Mirror to show us another way in, and I'm pretty sure the Duke isn't expecting one either.

"This could work," I say. "But is it wide enough? Show me the whole way through into the cave."

The Mirror proceeds to show Molly and me the entire trajectory through the crevice, down some tight passages, some steep drops, then finally into a maze of rear caverns that lead into the main cave.

"That looks tricky," she says. "But I think we can do it. I'll sketch a map out."

She finds some paper and a quill and proceeds to create a map and list of directions.

"And what about the Ruler?" she asks as she draws.

"What about her?" I ask. The truth is, my main concern is with the Duke. He lurks and prowls. He hunts and devours. He's just like one of the creatures, ripping the life out of everything he comes into contact with.

"She's the one who helped orchestrate the kidnapping, right? So shouldn't we do something about her?"

"Let's focus on Sir Jasper and the Duke for now. As far as I am concerned, the Duke is the mastermind behind this, and the Ruler is just another one of his pawns. If we succeed at rescuing Sir Jasper, then we can see about what to do."

"So, what's our plan? Just go down the crevice?"

"Do you think you are up for this, what with everything you went through yesterday?"

Molly nods. "But we will need horses if we are to make it all the way out to the sea caves," she adds.

"There are a few horses here. I saw stables in the back. Let's get ready and meet there as soon as possible."

She nods, and we run off to prepare for whatever lies ahead.

CHAPTER 39
Molly

My ribs ache with every breath. Sharp pains from my cuts and bruises remind me I'm in terrible shape. Yet, even if it's dreadful to move, attempting to find Sir Jasper is a hundred times better than lying in bed all day, wondering if Colin and the Head Keeper will survive the Duke.

I find a dress hanging in the closet and thread it on, then wrap myself in a thick cloak and cover my face with a big shawl. Now, more than ever, I need to keep my identity a secret. Will I ever not have to hide myself? I feel like that has been the story of my life, and after everything that happened last night, it's even worse.

On my way down to the stables, I find the kitchen and choose a knife to take with me. I hope I can use it to cut Sir Jasper free. As far as stables go, this one has five stalls, all five of which are full. When Colin arrives, we saddle three of the horses, two for us, and one for Sir Jasper—assuming we succeed.

Without any further discussion, we take off with our hoods drawn low, heading down a small road leading away from this part of town. Through the hustle and bustle of the city streets, I ride behind Colin, trying to blend in as best I can. Finally, the buildings thin out and we approach the outskirts of the city and the inner wall. Keepers don't track people leaving the city, but riding past them is still unnerving.

After we make it to the agricultural lands, we ride to the coastline. Time is slipping by, and the Duke is likely watching for us. This task feels almost impossible.

As we approach the rocky alcoves, we loop around to the back side. Even here, the Duke's Keepers patrol the whole area. We stop and loosely tie the horses in a grove of trees before they see us, and from there, walk a distance to move in closer.

Once the light of torches comes into view, we crouch down against a mound.

Then, Colin pulls out the Mirror.

"You brought it?" I can't believe he would do that.

"How else are we supposed to have a shot at succeeding?"

I can't argue, but the risk seems still too great.

"The Duke isn't leaving Sir Jasper's side," Colin says after looking into the Mirror. "As long as he hovers around him, we can't go into the cave. I was hoping we could sneak in there, and no one would even realize he was gone until it was too late."

"We could create a diversion to draw the Duke out. Do you want me to go down there? Considering they all think I'm dead, I could give them a pretty good scare. And, while I'm confusing them, you can head down to help Sir Jasper."

Colin glares at me fiercely while wrapping the Mirror back up and tucking it deep into his cloak.

"And then what?" he says. "What if they catch you?"

We sit, bunched up against the divot in the little hill, seemingly out of options. And soon enough, the horses begin neighing. Someone is coming close.

"I'm going to have to face the Duke," Colin finally says. "You find Sir Jasper, and I'll give you the Mirror, so the Duke doesn't have a chance at it."

But already, several of the Duke's Keepers are approaching. If we stay here, we will be found. Colin is struggling and taking too long to hand me the Mirror. We have to run. This might be my last chance to go before we are spotted.

"Just hide it," I tell Colin. I don't know if he hears me, but I'm already scurrying away. "I don't need it." I say as I run. Better that than be caught now.

This feels risky, but what choice does he have?

Just in time, I duck behind some bushes, while I see Colin bolt over the hill, headed toward the water. The Keepers keep walking the area, but don't seem to notice us.

I have no idea what Colin is planning on doing, and I am worried for him. Helping Sir Jasper should be my only focus, though, if it's the last thing I do. Without Sir Jasper keeping the Duke in check, who knows what the Ruler and the Duke duo will do to the cities.

I am going to have to time this right. How will I know if it's safe to approach Sir Jasper or when the Duke leaves? Hopefully, I won't mess this up.

By the sun's lowering place in the sky, my guess is that we have very little time until Sir Jasper drowns. Thick bushes and vines cover the entrance I am searching for, but eventually, I find the way in. I pull out my map and sneak into the crevice. Little by little, I climb down the rear side of the cavern. As I approach Sir Jasper's holding place, the path becomes trickier, especially given my sore ribs and inability to see more than a few feet in front of me. I just hope I don't end up wedged inside the confines of this cave forever.

When the way becomes narrower, I switch to a crawl, letting my hands and instincts guide me. As I continue forward, I think I hear something ahead of me. I stop to listen, but discern nothing. Maybe it was merely my imagination, or maybe it's the Duke and his Keepers still there. I can't tell.

Despite the increasing anxiety washing over me, I continue. When I finally come to a larger opening in the cavern, I conceal myself in a nook to wait and determine if anyone or anything is around. I tuck myself low and hold my breath. Despite the coolness of the cave, and the water rising over my legs, sweat trickles down the back of my neck, and my heart beats like a debt collector banging at the door. The cold sea can't help but remind me of everything I went through last night, but now is not the time to allow my thoughts to wander into the total depths of fear.

I think I hear something again. I pause and decide to count to sixty. Then, I creep out of hiding.

As I edge past formations of stalactites and stalagmites, I finally think I find the person I came here for. It must be Sir Jasper. He is blindfolded, but alone—at least, it appears so. I know he hears me approaching because he tilts his head my way. Already the water has risen higher, and my sloshing is loud as I move to find him.

"This cavern is already taken," he says. "You'll have to find somewhere else."

How could he make a joke at a time like this?

I slide in next to him and tap his shoulder.

"Guess who it is?" I whisper.

"Is it my favorite bread maker?" he asks, angling toward me. "I thought I heard someone coming."

I pull the cover down from his face. "I'm so happy I found you." I give him a massive hug.

"Still doing your good deeds under the cover of darkness, I see," he says with a warm smile.

I want to smile back, but our situation is still terrible.

"Colin is outside, with the Duke. We have to help him."

"He is?" Sir Jasper's features tighten. "So that's why that snake finally left me. I thought our conversation had bored him. I can imagine Colin will need our help."

I show him the map I made. "Let me untie you."

The Keepers wrapped many rounds of twine around the Head Keeper's wrists and ankles, which I manage to cut through with my kitchen knife. When Sir Jasper is finally free and standing on his own two feet, I can't help but give him another big squeeze.

"Now let's get out of here," Sir Jasper says.

The tide is rising fast. This cave is huge, and there are so many caverns and nooks and crannies. Already, the water is way above our knees.

I pull my map up high, preventing it from touching the water. I sure wish we had some light and that I had taken the Mirror. I can barely see anything, but Sir Jasper and I survey the cavern to identify our exit. Finally, I recognize the stalactites from my way in.

"Follow me," I tell Sir Jasper.

I retrace my steps to where I hid while listening for the Duke. After that, I guide Sir Jasper along the ragged edges of the cavern to the deep crevice we need to leave through. It is difficult to climb through the side of the cavern, especially with the ever-increasing aches of all my injuries, and this time, we are going up, and there are some steep sections of rock to climb. Sir Jasper is in excellent condition for his age, but I can tell it requires his entire focus, too.

The good thing is, somehow, after much diligent effort and many scrapes and tight squeezes, we manage to find our way.

"Hopefully the horses are still where I left them," I say. "They were being a bit noisy."

"Hmph," he says. "I guess it's worth a shot."

"This way," I tell him.

CHAPTER 40
Colin

The night sky drenches the cavern and the surrounding ocean with darkness, except for the eerie glow coming from the guards' fires and torches. Molly thinks I have come to create a diversion—and in a way, I have—but in truth, I see only one possible way forward to resolve this dilemma: I need to confront the Duke.

I don't have the chance to hide myself as I approach the cave because the Duke's Keepers see me and call out to him.

And there he is. My once-beloved mentor, who betrayed and used me, emerges from his cave. Hopefully, Molly can free Sir Jasper now.

I had dedicated my life to honoring the man before me. He had been like home to me. Two weeks ago, I would have given my life for him and believed I owed him everything. Now, he turns my blood icy cold.

The Duke raises his hands, moving closer. Slowly, he approaches me across the rocky terrain covered with driftwood.

"The young Colin has returned." I've never seen him smile so broadly. "Come here," he says.

He's trying to give me orders as he always has, and I'm so accustomed to following them that, even though every part of me is repulsed by him, it's difficult for me not to obey.

"If you want the Mirror, you'll have to come to me," I say. I try to sound confident, but my stomach tightens with anxiety, and my heart pounds hard.

"Sit with me and talk. I mean you no harm," he says as he points to a nearby log that has drifted ashore.

"You know I care about you," the Duke continues. "Being your mentor has been a great privilege. More than that, we have been family with ties thicker than blood. There's nothing I wouldn't do for you. I can help you."

I did not expect him to be so mild-mannered. His words have a mind-numbing power over me. If I hadn't seen the depth of his lies, I might have succumbed to his spell, like I used to.

"All you have ever done is to seek to destroy me and my family," I say. Has he forgotten he had his Keepers beat me just a few days ago?

The Duke hesitates before continuing, but otherwise his composure is practically flawless. "That is a misrepresentation of the circumstances. You haven't heard my side of the story."

He causes me to wonder, even if just for a fleeting moment, if I have misinterpreted anything. Could I be mistaken? Yet, I force myself to remember how his actions, however they might have first appeared, were for evil and for his own, selfish ambitions.

"What about everything we've been through together?" he continues.

As our eyes lock, it's as if I glimpse sickly eyes within him—and also a monstrous, yet emaciated form. Without a doubt, he is just like one of the creatures, and he is hungry. His eyes, mouth, and claws appear desperate to devour me.

"Why did you kill my parents?" I ask him. "I know it was you."

The Duke smiles weakly. "Your father became greedy and wouldn't allow the Keepers to use the Mirror. We tried to talk sense into him, but he was obsessed. He left me no other choice. But you are different, aren't you?"

Fiery fear pounds through my veins. I really hope that Molly has been able to help Sir Jasper out of the cave.

"And that's because you know that, in the end, the Mirror belongs to all the Keepers," he continues.

Suddenly, he bounds forward and grabs the front of my cloak. I hadn't realized how close we had come to each other.

"You will never have the Mirror," I say.

He puts the flames of his torch near my face and squeezes my arm. His Keepers surround me on every side, but they don't matter. I only have one objective: *him*. I try to appear calm, but my emotions seep out in a hundred little ways: my hands tremble, I sweat profusely, and I can't see straight.

"Where is it?" he asks.

My hand slips to my dagger, my fingers wrapping themselves around its handle.

You are a true Keeper. It's like I hear my father and Molly speaking. Even though they aren't here, their voices are crystal clear in my mind. The world around me appears to slow down, and I perceive every one of the Duke's emotions—his pain and fear—despite his advantage.

I lower my knife and, while the Duke is looking at it, I punch him in the face. Caught off guard, he fumbles long enough for me to hit him several times more. As the Duke falls backwards, his Keepers try to swarm me.

"Colin, your horse!" Molly shouts from the top of the nearby mounds and gallops toward me with Sir Jasper.

"She's alive?" one of the Keepers says.

"How?" asks another.

I take that moment to grab the torch the Duke has dropped, and swing it in a circle around me.

The Duke appears shocked at Molly's sight, but neither I nor the guards are prepared for his speed or determination. Exploding with power—his muscles, mind, and hatred working together in perfect unity—he grabs my dagger and drives it into me. Our bodies fold over, blood spilling down me and onto the earth below.

I take in the sight of the Duke with astonishment and shock. His knife hit the Mirror hidden in my cloak, not me. The blood isn't mine—it's the Duke's, from the punches he took to the face.

As I steady myself, I whisper in the Duke's ear, "I may never be as good as my father, but I might somehow manage to not become like you after all."

In one quick motion, I spin the Duke around, and hold the knife to his throat.

"If any one of you approaches, he dies," I shout to the Duke's Keepers. At least I learned that move from my monster of a mentor.

With that, the Keepers stand still, seemingly unsure how to proceed. Meanwhile, Molly and Sir Jasper approach with the horses.

"We have to take him with us," I shout.

Sir Jasper throws a cloak over the Duke's head and helps tie his hands. Then, we load him on to one of the horses with me behind him. I hate the idea of riding with him, but how else are we supposed to do this?

"You think you can win?" the Duke asks, as we gallop ahead. "My Keepers will stop you before you even make it to the first wall." His words are saturated with condescension. There is a part of me that still wishes I could just kill the Duke, here and now, and deliver him as a warning to the Ruler.

We ride off as fast as we can. When I glance over my shoulder, I thankfully don't see any of his Keepers pursuing us yet. But soon enough, I expect them to be right on our tail. And another problem is, I am unsure which way to go—except away.

As we gallop ahead, Sir Jasper rides up next to me and points forward, like he understands my predicament. I nod and he takes the lead. All I have to do is make it to wherever Sir Jasper is taking us.

As we travel fast through the agricultural lands to the city, it is unnerving having the Duke so close to me, like at any moment he could transform into a poisonous viper that will strike and kill me. Truthfully, I only ever imagined leaving here with Sir Jasper. Never did it occur to me that we would also have the Duke.

The Duke shifts in front of me.

"You have the Mirror, don't you?" he says.

I focus on the lights that line the wall ahead and try to prevent my body from tensing up, but a bitter taste fills my mouth. There is no need for me to respond to him, but I'm glad his hands are tied tight.

He chuckles. "You're fighting on the wrong side, Colin."

"You killed my parents," I say.

I can almost sense him smile. "How do you think Saint Michael and Saint Selaphiel continue to survive with such limited resources at our disposal?" My stomach churns. "We need more and more food," he continues, "and, therefore, more and more land. Otherwise, we die. That's why I had to take over other cities, but your father didn't understand. We needed more agricultural lands. Your parents lost sight of that."

I'm sick of listening to him. I hope we arrive soon. I should have gagged him. His words are always twisted. I can't listen to them anymore. Does he ever stop talking?

"The Ruler understands, though," he continues. "And that's why ultimately, Colin, you are going to lose this battle. The Mirror will be mine, and in the end, I will go down as the true Keeper and savior of our cities. You will eventually realize I am only faithfully doing what needs to be done."

I try my best to ignore him and whatever he says, block him out until, at long last, we go past the city wall. Having Sir Jasper with us makes our entrance into Saint Selaphiel much simpler.

As we travel down the cobblestone streets, people are watching and talking. Sir Jasper redirects us down a number of side alleys, until we arrive at the back of a tall wall and rear entryway to the Hall of Prayers.

Then, Sir Jasper whistles the loudest whistle I've ever heard. The whole neighborhood will know we're here now. In response, the Whittler, along with a dozen true Keepers, run out to meet us.

"Please lock him up," Sir Jasper says, pointing to the Duke.

"You can't lock me up," the Duke says.

Before the Keepers can take him, the Duke swings his bound hands around and wraps them around my neck, pulling me up against him, pressing into my throat, cutting my airway off.

"Hand me the Mirror and get off this horse. Then, I will let you live," he says.

"I would rather die," I tell him.

He doesn't have time to respond, though, because Molly swings around in front of us on her horse, snatches one of the Keepers' swords, and wields it like a fighting stick. It spins through the air and lands right on the center of the Duke's skull, barely missing me. When it hits, I hear a loud *thunk*, and the Duke collapses off the horse with me in tow.

Sir Jasper helps me as I untangle myself from my former mentor. In the chaos, I make eye contact with Molly, thankful for her intervention.

We did it.

"Are you all right?" I ask her. At the same time, I stuff my hands in my pockets and realize that, in the midst of the riding and the chaos, I'm somehow holding two vials of the Remedy. How did I get them? Did the Duke slip them to me in the chaos?

"I'm fine," Molly answers. "How are you?"

"Fine, too," I say, but I'm conflicted. Why do I have Remedy?

Sir Jasper is holding on to my horse for support, and tilts his head at me oddly, his face creased.

"What's the matter?" he asks.

I show him what I have.

He frowns and swings off his horse. When he approaches me, I hand him the vials.

"There are better ways. I know that now," I say. "The Duke thinks we'll need him, but we won't."

Meanwhile, the Keepers hoist the Duke away. He is carried through a doorway, then disappears. I imagine my former mentor being led down the maze of stone staircases I became familiar with just the previous day. I imagine him in front of a cell door as a guard pulls out a long chain of iron keys and locks him up inside a miserable, damp, and dirty cell, everything thick with darkness. But what will happen now?

"The Keepers are trustworthy, right?" I ask Sir Jasper, motioning to the door the Duke just was taken through.

"They have all been vetted by me and the Whittler," he replies. "But we must close the gates now and make sure his Keepers cannot come for him."

"Come with me," the Whittler says to me, and he directs me to the broad opening in the stone wall. He reaches for an iron ring. A matching ring is tucked within the stones of the other half of the entry. When he pulls on his ring, out surges an intricate iron gate. I follow his lead, and out slides my side of the gate. This metal work resembles that of the Straight Street bridge, like a forest made of iron.

"There is more to this gate than what meets the eye," the Whittler says to me. "Would you like to try to learn?"

"I would love to," I say.

The Whittler winks at me and continues about his business.

CHAPTER 41
Molly

With the good Keepers, Colin and I help close the gates. While I'm busy pulling them closed along with everybody else, I'm unexpectedly feeling a little empty. Despite all our victories, I wish Hugo was here and that I had had the chance to see my mother.

When we are done, everyone else heads indoors, but Colin and I linger outside. Snowflakes wisp around us, gentle and beautiful. Colin catches snowflakes and watches them as they melt. I rub my hands together for warmth.

"You look a little sad," he says.

"I guess I miss Hugo, and I wish I could have seen my mother."

"Now that the Duke is out of the way, I'm sure you'll see both of them soon."

I know he's right. And I may not have my brother and mother with me now, but I have other wonderful people, including him.

"Let's go find Sir Jasper," he says. "I saw him slip in there, and want to ask him something." He points at the Cathedral of Saint Selaphiel.

"In there?"

"Yes. After everything, that's where he chose to go."

"Aren't there higher priorities?"

"I guess not."

Inside the church, candles light not only the whole heart and altar, but also every pew. A handful of people are kneeling in prayer. Somewhere, someone is playing a stringed instrument. Whoever is in charge of decorations has gone above and beyond to celebrate the season because they have brought in full pine trees and arranged them throughout the cathedral so that they surround us on all sides. The mesmerizing ensemble of flickering candlelight and pines seemingly make the carved stone columns come alive, and the whole place smells like a forest. I breathe in the scent of pine, incense, and burning candles.

Normally, I would readjust the hood around my head and the scarf around my face to make sure no one can recognize me, but this time, I pull them down. I want to try to be me.

Sir Jasper is in prayer, at the back, in a dark corner. Colin and I go kneel beside him. I bow my head, close my eyes, and give thanks. Sir Jasper is safe, the Duke is locked up, and Colin and I are not fleeing for our lives.

"I'm glad you came," Sir Jasper says.

"How are you doing?" we ask.

"I'm having a little bit of a hard time," Sir Jasper says. "I can't imagine how difficult these last days have been for the two of you."

"I have a question," Colin says.

Sir Jasper glances at him.

"Can you read our minds with your glasses?"

Sir Jasper laughs. "They are crafted by the same artists who created the Mirror—the Whittler's family. They don't show me everything in someone's mind, but whatever is relevant to what I inquire about. For example, I can see whether someone is telling me the truth."

He glances at me. He must have known I was innocent all along, then.

"Do you know about my mother?" I ask, tucking my hands under my armpits, hugging myself. "Did she really have to leave us?"

The Master Keeper shifts in his pew, causing a shadow to obscure his face. I wish I could put on his mysterious glasses to find out what he is thinking.

"I find it helpful not to assume the worst of people. Your mother may not have had much choice in everything that happened," Sir Jasper says.

"But she abandoned Hugo and me."

"The Duke questioned her relentlessly," Sir Jasper says. "He thought your mother would know where your father hid the Mirror, and he was always after her. The further she stayed away from you, the less the Duke would bother you. Your mother might have been able to go about things differently if she hadn't been through so much herself. Anyone in her shoes would have had a difficult time. Your mother may have made mistakes, but she loves you."

We sit in silence for a little while. I want to keep asking him questions, but maybe Colin and I should leave him alone now.

"I'm sorry we interrupted your prayers," I say.

"I'm glad you did," he says. "Now good night. I'll see you in the morning."

It was nice having that time with him and Colin, and as I go on my way, sorting out my sleeping arrangements, joy washes over me.

CHAPTER 42
Colin

I lie in my bed, processing all that happened. What will happen to the Duke now? If the Ruler can't be trusted, who will govern the cities? Whatever happened to the other five lost cities? What will happen to Saint Raphael now?

I pull the Mirror out, about to start asking it about Saint Raphael, when someone knocks on my door. I conceal the Mirror under my pillow, and when I open up, it's the Whittler.

"Good evening," he says, his eyes creased up from his big smile. I have so many questions about this man and who he is, too. "I know you have already had a very full day, but the Keepers need your assistance."

"Sure. What is it?" I ask, already putting my boots back on.

"The Ruler," he says. "She could be coming for the Duke and for the Mirror, but we don't know. We need information. Can you help us?"

Obviously, he means for me to help them research the situation with the Mirror. How should I go about doing this? What parameters should I set? How did my father do this?

"I'd be happy to check for you," I say, unsure of what precedent I am setting for myself. While I don't like being requested to use the Mirror like this, the future of our cities is at stake.

"Thank you. Please come find us in the library when you are ready."

Before he leaves, I can't help but place a hand on his shoulder to stop him. "I'm just wondering," I say. "Since your family made the Mirror, how come you don't make more?"

"Who says we haven't?"

"So, were you serious about teaching me?"

"I have been searching for an apprentice," he says. "I have no children of my own."

I'm blown away. "Thank you," I say, but that hardly feels enough.

He smiles. "I am grateful, too."

After he leaves, I pull the Mirror back out. "Show me the Ruler."

The image in the Mirror ripples to the Ruler. She is pacing back and forth in what appears to be a bedroom. She seems conflicted, not ready to come after the Duke. If the Ruler is anything like I was, the Duke has brainwashed her into thinking all sorts of lies.

A cloaked person approaches her. I cannot see their face, but they are talking at length with her.

"What are they saying?" I ask the Mirror.

"Forget about the Duke," I hear the person say. "You don't need him anymore. Once we have the Mirror, we can do everything he did and more. Just find a way to get the Mirror. I'll take care of the Remedy."

"Who is she talking to?" I ask. The image ripples, and when I see the face appear before me, it's the Ruler's young brother, the one the Duke had been speaking to in front of that plum door.

CHAPTER 43
Molly

The bedroom walls are covered with light green wallpaper, with golden and dark green leafy designs, and there is a comfy chair by my own little fireplace. I'd love to enjoy it, but unfortunately, someone is knocking at my door. "We need you to come now," someone says.

"Just a moment," I reply. Don't they realize how sore I am?

I pull up my hair and splash my face with water at a little sink on the side of my room. I almost throw on my hooded cloak, but leave it behind.

In the hallway is the man Colin was speaking with last night—his wild hair and twinkling eyes are unforgettable. He leads me up several flights of stairs into a library. A stained-glass window runs the full length of the room, but because it's night, no light comes through. I imagine that, during the day, it must bathe the whole room in dozens of patches of color. A handful of people talk around a large table, candlelight flickering between them.

Sir Jasper notices me first. When he stands to greet me, the room stills.

Across from me are two women, likely just a little older than I am. The one across from me wears a beautifully carved hair ornament shaped like a bird; the other has braids so long they disappear under the table. Next to her is a young man entirely focused on eating some food.

"Molly helped save my life last night. Molly, these are my most trusted Keepers in Saint Selaphiel," Sir Jasper says.

My heart tightens. I wish I were one of them, but that's a dream I need to relinquish.

"We're glad you are here," a freckled young man with dimples and a pleasant grin says. "It's nice to meet you."

When I sit down at the table, one of the women pours me a cup of something warm to drink. A few moments later, the Whittler re-enters the room with Colin. He's all cleaned up and freshly shaven, but looks exhausted. As he glances around the room, he sees me and smiles. My heart flickers with joy as he comes to sit beside me.

"This is Colin. I'm sure you know who he is. He will be updating us on what is happening with the Ruler," Sir Jasper says. Everyone around the table stills, and uneasy tension saturates the air.

"She is not coming for the Duke. Her brother seems to want to take over for him," Colin says. He tells them about the Ruler and her brother speaking in the Mirror about their plans. Sir Jasper then takes the lead, and they begin outlining an action plan.

As they talk, Colin leans into me. "Come with me," he says, tugging on my sleeve. He picks up one of the little candles in its holder.

"We'll be right back," he tells Sir Jasper.

Though the meeting continues, I follow Colin into an empty side room. The walls are lined with books, with one section devoted to scrolls. A ladder provides access to higher shelves.

"I have something for you," Colin says.

He pulls out a brown paper parcel.

"What is it?" I ask.

"This is actually not what I'm going to give you. It's connected to it."

Colin holds the package in his hands, almost as if he is hesitant to open it in front of me, even though he is the one who called me in here. When he finally opens it, I see a box engraved and ornamented with intricate leaves and birds.

"Wow! It's beautiful," I say.

"I made this box for Uncle Felix," he says. "This was my contender gift to him."

I'm stunned. "You made this? It's amazing."

"The Whittler returned it to me. He said Sir Jasper brought it to him after the librarians found it in the library, where I had hidden it."

Colin steps closer, as if he is going to share a secret with me. "There's something I need to give you," he says. Then, he reaches into his shirt and, from under his layers, pulls out two keys strung around his neck. I had seen them before, but never paid much attention. He unties one of the keys and lets it play through his fingers. "It would make me happy to know you had one of these," he says. "Do you happen to still have your ribbon?"

I pull the sky blue ribbon from my satchel.

He threads the key onto it. "These are the keys to my uncle's box. It requires two. You will have one, and I will have the other."

He shows me how we unlock the box together. I marvel at the details that unfold as we open it up.

"The Mirror will be guarded by both of us. I really need your help with this, at least until we make it back to Saint Michael. It is hard to keep track of who's after the Mirror." He pulls the Mirror from his shirt and slides it in the box.

"You trust me?" My heart is thundering.

He ties the ribbon around my neck. "There is no one I trust more."

CHAPTER 44
Molly

A homeless looking fellow is sitting on the steps of Saint Michael's Cathedral. I can't see his face because of his hood, but by the tilt of his head, I know he sees me from the other side of the street. His mannerisms are the familiar ones I came here for.

He removes his hood, revealing deep wrinkles in his features and dirt matted hair. Finally, our eyes meet. They are bloodshot and exhausted, squinting at me with curiosity.

As I come close, the smell emanating from him is pungent. My brother has obviously been through hell, but he's smiling now.

For a few moments, we take each other in, then I pull him into my arms in a huge hug. I haven't seen Hugo in too long, and a few tears find their way down my cheeks.

"I'm sorry I couldn't come for you earlier," I say. "I tried everything I could."

"How are you still alive?" My brother's voice sounds strained and steeped in confusion. "They told me you died."

"The Duke did throw me over the cliffs, but Colin and Sir Jasper helped me. You didn't know?"

"No one told me anything." Hugo's face puckers like he's eaten a sour grape. "They let me out a few days ago, but I had nothing and nowhere to go. I've been too weak to really do anything except sit here and think. But why would Colin help you?"

"He's different now, and he has new mentors. And another crazy thing is that it was the Duke who killed Colin's family, not our father. Everything we thought was true isn't." I consider telling him about the Mirror, but that news might be too much.

Hugo's head tilts as he processes what I am saying, and anger begins to permeate his features; his expression stiffens and his eyes harden.

"Don't think about that right now. The Duke is in prison. Can I buy you a warm soup, though?" I ask him.

"I guess a hot soup would be nice."

"And we can talk about happier things, like the fact that I discovered the most marvelous village in the forest where, believe it or not, they have guardian reindeer. I can't wait to show you. I think you will love it there!"

"A wilderness village with reindeer? Huh…well, then I guess anything is possible."

He stands with difficulty, then leans into me to walk. When I wrap my arms around him to support him, he lowers his head to my shoulder, and for the first time ever, he starts to cry.

"Everything will be different now," I tell him. "You'll see. Our lives are going to be beautiful."

ACKNOWLEDGEMENTS

When I set out to write a book in February of 2015, I had no idea what I was signing myself up for. The only way I was able to finish writing *A Tale of Two Sparrows* (originally *Mirror of Sparrows*) was because of the many family, friends, and mentors who came alongside me. The following people not only helped me stay motivated, but also provided tremendous guidance, kindness, and thoughtfulness. I am forever grateful for their support.

Max, Maile, Skye, and Cruz—you always believed in me and have put up with way too many conversations about story structure—you are the best; Mama—you relentlessly encourage me and envision the best for me; Papa—thank you for challenging me to be consistent with my writing and encouraging me. Holly and Angie—our storytelling adventures have been an amazing gift. Jan, Daniel, SeonMi, Alessandra, Aleya, Malia, Ari, Elisha, and Gracie—I cherish the time, enthusiasm, and insights you have sown into the story.

I am indebted to Ellen Brock for her knowledge and priceless insights in the first stages. I also would like to recognize the RevPit community and Jenni Chappelle, the SCBWI Hawaii community and the Plucky Pueo writing group, the Hawaii NaNoWriMo community and Mitchell Dwyer, Chris Tebbetts, Stephanie Cardel, and most recently, Nicole Evans for helping me with line editing. I also want to remember the high school teachers who first encouraged my storytelling and writing, Mrs. Lindsey and Mrs. Litvinas.

Most of all, I am grateful to God and the way He has used storytelling, imagination, and writing to enrich my life in ways more incredible than I ever could have imagined.